PRAISE FOR
Baby-Sitting Is a Dangerous Job

"Electrifying suspense."
—*Publishers Weekly*

"A solid adventure with more than
a few spine-tingling moments."
—*Booklist*

**DON'T MISS THESE OTHER
WILLO DAVIS ROBERTS MYSTERIES:**

Surviving Summer Vacation
The View from the Cherry Tree
Megan's Island
The Kidnappers
Hostage
Scared Stiff
The Pet-Sitting Peril
What Could Go Wrong?
Secrets at Hidden Valley

Baby-Sitting Is a Dangerous Job

WILLO DAVIS ROBERTS

ALADDIN

NEW YORK LONDON TORONTO SYDNEY NEW DELHI

ALADDIN

An imprint of Simon & Schuster Children's Publishing Division
1230 Avenue of the Americas, New York, New York 10020
This Aladdin paperback edition April 2016
Text copyright © 1985 by Willo Davis Roberts
Cover illustration copyright © 2016 by Jessica Handelman
Also available in an Aladdin hardcover edition.
All rights reserved, including the right of reproduction
in whole or in part in any form.
ALADDIN is a trademark of Simon & Schuster, Inc., and related logo
is a registered trademark of Simon & Schuster, Inc.
For information about special discounts for bulk purchases,
please contact Simon & Schuster Special Sales at 1-866-506-1949
or business@simonandschuster.com.
The Simon & Schuster Speakers Bureau can bring authors
to your live event. For more information or to book an event contact
the Simon & Schuster Speakers Bureau at 1-866-248-3049
or visit our website at www.simonspeakers.com.
Cover designed by Jessica Handelman
Interior designed by Mike Rosamilia
The text of this book was set in New Century Schoolbook.
Manufactured in the United States of America 0316 OFF
2 4 6 8 10 9 7 5 3 1
Library of Congress Control Number 2015957566
ISBN 978-1-4814-3705-9 (hc)
ISBN 978-1-4814-3704-2 (pbk)
ISBN 978-1-4814-3706-6 (eBook)

Chapter One

I knew the minute I saw the Foster kids that I wasn't going to like being their baby-sitter.

There were three of them. Shana was the little one, about two and a half, and she was cute. I thought maybe she'd be all right. She had soft blonde hair and big blue eyes, and she said my name, plain as anything, right after me when her mother asked me what it was. "Darcy Ann Stevens," Shana echoed, and leaned against my leg.

"And do they call you Darcy Ann, or just Darcy?" Mrs. Foster asked, smiling. Only she wasn't just *Mrs.*, she was a psychiatrist, and my friend Irene said everybody called her *doctor*. I wasn't sure how I was supposed to address her, so I hadn't called her anything at all.

"Just Darcy," I said.

I looked at the middle one, whose name was Melissa. She was four, and she was cute, too; her brown hair curled, but she stuck out her lower lip and looked at me with those big dark eyes and said, "I don't want you for a sitter."

Mrs./Dr. Foster smiled again. "Don't be rude, dear. Of course you're going to like Darcy as a sitter. And this, Darcy, is Jeremy. He's six."

Jeremy, too, had dark hair and the same dark eyes. When his mother looked away from him, he stuck his tongue out at me. He didn't say anything.

"I understand you've had quite a bit of experience baby-sitting, Darcy," Mrs./Dr. Foster said. She turned directly toward me on the big oatmeal-colored couch, and Jeremy, behind her back, stuck his thumbs in his ears and wiggled his fingers at me. "You're how old? Fourteen?"

"Well, nearly," I said. "I'm thirteen and a half." I was only stretching it by three months. "Yes, I've been babysitting since I was eleven."

"Eleven," she echoed. "That's very young to start. You must be quite mature for your age."

"Yes," I agreed. "Everybody says so. It probably

2

comes from having two little brothers. I helped take care of them, too."

Now Jeremy had a finger in each corner of his mouth, stretching it to make a grotesque face. Melissa looked at him and copied his actions. I was already having second thoughts about this.

In the first place, I'd never taken on *three* kids before. And none of the children I'd baby-sat had ever lived in a place like this, either.

"Well," Mrs./Dr. Foster said. "Your references are certainly good ones." She handed the letters back to me, and I rested them on my knees. "Shall we see you tomorrow afternoon, then, Darcy? Say at one o'clock? I can't tell you how happy we are to have found someone reliable to see to the children while Mrs. Murphy is having her root canals done. I'm sure they're going to love you."

Jeremy had his tongue out again, wiggling it like a serpent's tongue; I wouldn't have been surprised if there had been a little steam with it, or a blast of fire. Melissa watched him to see what he did and imitated it a moment later.

Mrs./Dr. Foster stood up, so I did, too.

"We didn't discuss pay, did we?" Mrs./Dr. Foster said, hesitating as we reached the front door. She named an hourly rate that was twice what anybody else paid me, and I swallowed the words I'd almost been ready to say. *Maybe you'd better find someone older, more experienced with three kids.* "Will that be satisfactory?" she asked. "Of course, we always pay a bonus for a job well done."

A bonus. On top of twice my normal hourly rates. I ignored Jeremy's wicked little face and forced myself to smile. "I'll be here tomorrow at one," I agreed.

My brother Tim was waiting for me at the curb in his beat-up old Volkswagen. He leaned across and opened the door for me—because it sticks, not because he was polite—and I slid in.

"Well, get the job?" he asked.

"Yes. I start tomorrow afternoon."

He put the car in gear and turned the key, but didn't drive away. He was looking at the Foster house. "Pretty ritzy place. What's it like inside?"

"Fancy," I said. "There's a swimming pool out back. I saw it through the patio doors."

He lifted his eyebrows. Tim looks like the rest of us in the Stevens family. We all, except Mom, have red hair and freckles. Her hair is auburn, and I keep hoping mine will get darker when I get older, so it will look like hers. "They going to let you swim in it?"

"I guess while I'm baby-sitting I can swim if I want to," I said. "Nobody mentioned it."

"How'd you like the kids?"

I made a face. "Little brats, I think. Still it's only for a couple of hours a day on the afternoons when the housekeeper, Mrs. Murphy, goes to the dentist for root canal work. I should be able to stand it for a few hours a day. And she said there'd be a bonus if I did a good job."

"Sounds good. Maybe you'll make enough to get your own stereo on this one job instead of taking all summer," Tim said.

"I hope so. I think I'm going to earn it." I told him about the two older ones making faces at me, and how Melissa had said she didn't want me for a sitter.

Tim laughed and eased the car away from the curb. "I can't bring you over every day and pick you up. You'll have to ride your bike."

5

"Okay," I said. I swiveled around in the seat to look back at the big Spanish-style house I'd just come out of. We don't live in the part of the country where Spanish-style houses are plentiful; it really stood out in this neighborhood of huge, expensive houses.

And because I turned to look, I saw the car that pulled out behind us. It was black, almost as beat-up as Tim's Volkswagen, not the kind of car you'd expect in this part of town. The sun reflected off the windshield, so I couldn't see who was driving, or how many people were in it.

"I think we're being followed," I joked.

"It's because we look like we're rich," Tim said, glancing in the rearview mirror. "I mean, that's who they'd follow to rob, right? Somebody with a classy car."

"Right," I said, and settled back for the ride home. The funny thing was, when we turned off onto our own street, that black car was still behind us. I saw it when we went around the corner.

"Tim," I began, but he wasn't listening. He was looking toward our house, a big old-fashioned place with a veranda across the front of it, where three teenaged boys were sitting on the steps drinking pop out of cans.

"Hey, the gang's here. We're supposed to be going out to the river to swim. It's lucky your interview didn't take any longer, because if I'd missed going, I'd have disowned you."

Since he disowned me about twice a day, that wasn't too upsetting. I did wonder about the car, though. When we bumped into the driveway, I craned my neck to see where the other car went.

It didn't stop, but kept on right past our house. There were two men in it; I couldn't make out any more than that.

I had to wait for Tim to open the door before I could get out. The guys on the steps waved and yelled, and Tim got out and trotted toward them.

I stood for a minute, looking after the mysterious black car. It traveled slowly along to the next corner and turned as if to go back toward State Street, which is the main street in Marysville, the one we'd just turned off.

Just somebody driving around, maybe lost, I decided. After all, why would anybody follow *us*?

I went past the boys and into the house. Inside I made myself a peanut butter and jelly sandwich and forgot about the car. It didn't have anything to do with me. How could it?

Chapter Two

"What's she like?" my friend Irene asked. She sprawled across my bed, eating an apple. (If we'd been at her house, the snacks would have been Milky Ways or Hershey Big Block bars; *my* mom thinks even the stuff kids eat between meals should be nutritious, so we usually get fruit or raw carrots or something like that.) "I mean, I know what she *looks* like, she's pretty elegant, and I've seen her driving that gorgeous big Lincoln, but what's she really *like*?"

"I only saw her for a few minutes," I said. "And I kept looking at her house—I never was in a place like that before—and the kids kept making faces at me behind her back. Come on, walk to the store with me. I'm supposed to cook supper tonight, and we're out of onions for the stew."

Irene dragged herself reluctantly off the bed. She likes coming to my house where we can talk privately in my bedroom; she shares *her* room with two sisters, and there's no privacy at all. At least in a family where you're the only girl, you get a room to yourself.

Mine was quite nice, all done in green and white, because Mom said green would be prettiest with my red hair and make my eyes look greener. Irene's hair's black, and her eyes are dark brown, but she's so pretty she looks great against any background.

As usual, she was wearing jeans and a T-shirt—a yellow one with a splashy red rose on it. She thought the rose kept people from noticing that she was still pretty flat in that area, but I thought it called attention to it. Still, with her face, it didn't seem to matter too much that she was developing more slowly than I was. Once the boys saw her face, they kept looking.

We clattered down the stairs, past the room where my brothers Bobby and Jimmy were doing the cleaning up Mom had insisted they do today if they were going camping over next weekend. Jimmy was cramming stuff under his bed, and Bobby was complaining that he couldn't get the closet door closed if he put the balls and bats in there on top of the tennis rackets and Tim's bowling bag. "Why can't Tim keep his junk in his own room?" Bobby wanted to know.

We were gone before I heard what Jimmy answered. We dropped our apple cores in the garbage before we went out into the sunny afternoon. Tim and his buddies were gone, in someone else's car; Tim's old Volks had been left behind.

Irene ran a hand over one of the battered fenders as we walked past it. She's had a crush on Tim as long as I can remember, and even his car evoked a long sigh from her, but anybody only thirteen is a baby to Tim.

"I wish I could get a summer job," she said, taking her hand off Tim's car, and we walked across the street.

"I may give you this one, if those kids are as bratty as I think they're going to be," I told her, half-seriously. "I've taken care of *one* bratty kid, remember Freddie Cyphers? And I've taken care of two reasonably *good* kids at a time, the Martino girls. But I've never tried it with three brats at once." I reconsidered that and amended, "Well, two brats and one cutie. Though I didn't see enough of Shana to be sure what she's like. She may be as spoiled as the other two."

Irene shrugged. It seemed to me that she shrugged more than she used to. "I'll pass, if they're brats. I heard Dr. Foster doesn't believe in spanking kids. You're supposed to use psychology on them, instead."

I laughed. "I suppose being raised in a family of six redheads might pass for a course in psychology." Underneath, though, I felt a little bit uneasy. My folks used psychology on us, when they thought about it, but when that didn't work they reverted to old-fashioned methods of discipline, which had included paddling when we were smaller.

We got the onions at the store, and I got enough extra milk to make pudding for supper, and we were on our way home when Irene said, "Don't look now, Darcy, but I think we have a couple of admirers."

Irene is always thinking we have admirers.

All a boy has to do is glance in our direction, and she thinks he's stricken with us. None of them has ever asked us for a date, so it's hard to tell. Neither Mom nor Mrs. Pappagoras would allow us to go out with boys yet, anyway. Irene's mother says when she's fifteen, and my mom isn't committing herself yet; it depends on how mature I am, she says, and she doesn't mean how well my figure is coming along. I didn't get excited when she said we had admirers, figuring it was just her wishful thinking again.

"Look. That car parked there when we went in the store, and it's still there. They haven't gotten out or anything. Just be casual, look across the street, under that big tree."

I looked, of course. Slowly, casually, the way she suggested. And stubbed my toe on the curb, so the sack split when I nearly fell, and an onion rolled out into the street.

"Oh, classy, Darce," Irene told me. "I'm sure they're impressed with our grace and beauty now."

I went back for the onion, absent-mindedly. "It's the same car," I said, thinking aloud.

"Same car as what?" She shot a surreptitious

glance toward the black car, squared her shoulders to make the best of the yellow T-shirt, and pretended not to be interested in the car under the oak tree.

"The same one I saw earlier today when we left the Foster place. It followed us home and drove back out onto State Street."

I'll say one thing for Irene, she's not the type to let petty jealousy ruin a friendship. "Darcy, maybe you really do have an admirer! Did he follow you, for sure?"

"I don't know. It looks like the same car. I didn't notice the license number, though." I stopped and turned around, pretending to be looking past the car at some kids on the sidewalk. I didn't even know them, but I waved, not caring if they thought I was crazy. I wanted to get the number off that license plate.

"Who is it?" Irene asked, turning around too.

"I don't know. Have you got a pencil? The license number is 823 7AV."

She didn't have anything to write with, and neither did I, but Irene repeated the number as we turned and kept on walking. "Eight-two-three, seven A V. It almost rhymes, we should be able to remember it. Eight-two-three, seven A V."

"There are two guys in it," I said, when I'd repeated the number too. "I couldn't see them very well, it was too shady there. Young though, weren't they?"

I shifted the sack, hugging it against my chest so the onions wouldn't fall out again. "Come on, I need to get home and start supper so it'll be done when Mom gets home from work. It's Dad's bowling night, so they'll want to eat on time."

We were to be delayed once more, however. As we approached our corner—I wanted to turn and look to see if the black car was still there, but I didn't quite dare, for some reason—a familiar black-and-white police cruiser eased along the curb and stopped just ahead of us.

"Clancy," I said, thinking it was a friend of my brother Tim's, but it wasn't Clancy. This was a new officer, one we'd never seen.

I felt Irene going into her terrific posture act beside me, and heard her murmur. "Ummm, is he ever cute!"

Mom says Irene is boy crazy, but I had to

agree with her. The new cop didn't look much older than Tim, and he had brown curly hair and a nice face.

"Hi," he said.

We've been taught not to talk to strangers, but cops didn't count as strangers. At least I didn't think they did.

"Hi," we both answered, and stopped to look through the open window of the patrol car.

"Either one of you happen to be named Diana? Diana Hazen, maybe?"

I realized then he was looking at the gold-colored barrette in my hair, in the shape of a D. I shook my head. "No. I'm Darcy Stevens, and this is my friend, Irene Pappagoras."

"If you're looking for Diana Hazen," Irene said, before I could continue, "that must mean she's run away again."

The young officer consulted a paper on a clipboard. "Diana Hazen, age thirteen. You know her?"

"We're all in the same grade, but she's in a different homeroom," Irene offered. "She runs away all the time."

"She does?" he looked at his paper as if

expecting to find evidence of that there. "Do you know where she usually goes?"

Irene shrugged, and this time she wasn't doing it for effect. "She never goes very far. They always find her. Maybe the next time you find her, you shouldn't take her home. Maybe you should find out why she runs away so often."

His face was friendly, interested, intelligent. "You know why she runs away?"

"Because her dad's mean to her," I said, at the same time as Irene said, "She hates it at home. They hit her."

The officer, who wore an identification badge that said "Chris Roberts," had keen hazel eyes. "You sure of that?" he asked.

"That's what she said, when we asked why she had the bruises," I told him. We didn't know Diana very well, because she was never allowed to attend school parties or games or anything. But Irene and I had both been there when someone had asked her about the black-and-blue marks.

"I saw finger marks on her arm, once," Irene said. "Where her dad grabbed her. She doesn't talk about it, much, but I'm pretty sure it's true, they hit her."

"Do you know if she ever talked to anybody at school about it, being mistreated? Teachers, or the school nurse?"

"Not that we know of," Irene answered. "If anybody asked Mr. Hazen about it, he'd probably just hurt her worse as soon as they were gone. So why would she tell? Especially since the police always take her home."

He took a pen out of his shirt pocket and held it poised over the paper on the clipboard. "In case I want to talk to you young ladies again about this, could I have your names, addresses, and phone numbers?"

We gave them to him, and he waved a hand at us and drove off. Irene giggled. "Do you realize a man has finally asked for our phone numbers?"

I laughed, too, and then I turned to look after the police car.

It was just turning a corner, beyond the store.

The black car was gone.

Chapter Three

I rode my bike up the Fosters' driveway at five minutes to one the next afternoon and looked around for a place to park it. It wasn't the kind of house where a bicycle would look right on the lawn or leaning against the front porch. Actually, it wasn't a porch, just a roof over dark red tiles inside the Spanish-style arches across the front of the house, and I decided I'd better take the bike in there under the roof. I didn't want anybody to come along and steal it.

I rang the bell and waited, feeling a bit fluttery in the stomach. Freddie Cyphers was a little demon, but he was a lot smaller than I was, being only five, and there was only one of him. The Martino kids were girls, two and three; and if you read them stories and fed them periodically, they seldom caused any problems at all.

The Foster kids were going to be a new ball game altogether.

The door swung inward, and a plump, gray-haired lady stepped backward to let me enter. "I take it you're Darcy? The new sitter?"

"That's right," I said, and tried to look confident.

"I'm Mrs. Murphy. I have about twenty minutes before I leave for the dentist's office, so I'll show you around a bit. The children are playing in the backyard; they're looking forward to having you here while I'm gone."

I'll bet they are, I thought, and remembered Jeremy sticking out his tongue and gesturing at me with his thumbs in his ears.

"Ordinarily, they'd have had lunch before this, but Jeremy cut himself this morning and I had to take him to the emergency room for some stitches, so we got behind. I'm sure you can fix them something. There's tuna mixed in a bowl in the refrigerator, and fruit. Eat whatever you want yourself, of course."

"I just had my own lunch," I told her. "Thank you."

Tuna fish, I thought. It seemed like in a

house as big and fancy as this one, they'd have something different from what the kids had for lunch at our house.

"This is the living room, of course," Mrs. Murphy said, indicating the room at the side of the wide, tiled entrance hall, where I'd sat on the oatmeal-colored sofa for my interview. "Usually I get the children to play somewhere besides here. Dr. Foster likes this room to be tidy when she comes home."

I nodded, understanding. I could imagine the kids getting peanut butter and jelly on those pale sofas or the cream-colored carpeting. When I'd told Mom about that carpet, she'd raised her eyebrows and said, "With three kids?" in an incredulous voice.

We paused before an open doorway. "This is Mr. Foster's study. There's no reason for the children to be in there, either, nor in the master bedroom."

I peeked into the rooms, seeing walls of books and dark paneling in the study, a broad expanse of deep blue velvety carpet and a king-sized bed with a quilted white silk spread in the bedroom. I could understand why they wouldn't want the kids to play in those places, but I noted the housekeeper hadn't said they weren't *allowed* in those rooms, only that it was better if they stayed out of them. I hoped that wasn't a clue that nobody *made* these kids do anything they didn't want to do, or kept them from doing what you didn't want them to do.

"This is Jeremy's room," Mrs. Murphy said, and I looked in there, too.

There was no resemblance to the room my little brothers shared. There were twin beds with bright red spreads, a desk, two dressers, bookshelves, a toybox made to look like a train with four cars, and a whole wall of open shelves that held trucks, trains, teddy bears, a miniature farm, and about everything else I remembered seeing in Sears' Christmas catalog.

Everything was neat and in its place. I could even see under the beds, and there wasn't so much as a discarded sock visible, let alone the toys and books and records and orange peelings my brothers had under their beds.

Mrs. Murphy continued the tour. "This is

Melissa's room, and Shana's is just across the hallway."

They were much like Jeremy's room, except that Melissa's was blue and white, and Shana's was pink and white, and the toys ran more to dolls and stuffed animals; in Melissa's there was the most elaborate dollhouse I'd ever seen, standing on a table of its own so you could walk all the way around it. Even though I was past the age for dollhouses, I felt a twinge of envy.

"The playroom is back here," Mrs. Murphy said. "The children spend most of their time here, or in the back yard, if the weather's nice."

The playroom was about the size of half the ground floor of our house. The carpet was a frosted dark brown, which seemed to indicate that the decorator hadn't been a complete idiot about young children; and the room had a rocking horse, a table with a set of electric trains, a music player along one wall, and all around the place more books, stuffed toys, and games than our school has in the kindergarten. There was a real rowboat, with cushions in it, and a playhouse I was sure Jeremy could

23

stand up in. Through its windows I saw minia-ture furniture as nice as the stuff in the rest of the real house, except that it was smaller.

Wow! Lucky kids, I thought.

We'd made almost a circle through the house. Mrs./Dr. Foster had a study, too, and there was a formal dining room with a crystal chandelier and murals on the walls, and a smaller family dining area, and a kitchen in pale wood with gold and white vinyl floor and counter tops and every appliance I'd ever heard of—and some I hadn't. Beyond the kitchen was a utility room; and though she didn't show it to me, Mrs. Murphy said there was a recreation room downstairs with a pool table, a sauna, and exercise machines.

"It's time for me to go," the housekeeper said, consulting her watch. "I'll probably be back around four. The children are right out there. Oh, Dr. Foster said she forgot to ask you—can you swim?"

"Yes," I said, still sort of overwhelmed by the house, trying to memorize it all to tell Irene about it.

"Good. The children are allowed to swim

whenever they like, as long as they have a swimmer in the pool with them. Good-bye, then, I'll see you this afternoon."

When she was gone, I stood for a minute in the middle of the kitchen, almost wishing I was the one who'd gone to the dentist instead of Mrs. Murphy.

What was the matter with me? All I had to do was keep three little kids from killing themselves, or each other, or me, until Mrs. Murphy came back.

The kids looked up when I went out through the patio doors into the back yard. As I'd expected, it too was oversized, and there was a six-foot board fence around it.

Shana, the little one, was playing in a sandbox, spooning up sand into a bucket. As I approached, Jeremy came along and kicked the yellow plastic pail, sending it contents flying all over his sister.

I expected her to start crying, but she didn't. She snatched up the pail and hit him on the leg with it.

"You stop that, Jeremy!"

He paid no attention to her, coming to a

halt instead before me. "We told you we didn't want you for a sitter," he said.

"I want you for a sitter," Melissa decided. "So does Shana, don't you, Shana?"

The two year old looked me over, then nodded. "I'm hungry. Let's eat in shicken."

"Mrs. Murphy said there was tuna fish for sandwiches," I told them. "She didn't say anything about chicken."

Melissa reached for the younger girl's hand. "She means in the kitchen. *Shicken* means either kitchen or chicken."

"Oh. Well, shall we go get something to eat? We could even bring our sandwiches back out here in the sunshine, if you want."

"I don't want tuna fish sandwiches," Jeremy said. He was actually an angelic-looking little boy, very handsome, when he wasn't sticking his tongue out. There were several stitches in his left hand, made with black thread. "I want bacon and tomato."

He saw me looking at his injured hand and he held it up so I could see it better. "We were playing Jack be nimble, Jack be quick, with a pop bottle. I kicked it over accidentally and it broke. When I fell down, I got cut, and we had to go to the hospital."

"Jer'my bleeded all over," Shana contributed.

"He cried," Melissa added.

"Not very much," Jeremy said quickly. "Come on, I'm hungry."

We walked into the house, and I told them, "Mrs. Murphy didn't say anything about bacon and tomato sandwiches."

"I can fix them," Jeremy said, seeming to have forgotten he'd said he didn't want me there. "I can cook the bacon in the microwave, the way Mrs. Murphy does. It's easy that way, and the grease doesn't pop all over you and burn you."

He was already into the mammoth refrigerator, hauling out bacon.

I looked at him uneasily. "I don't know anything about cooking with microwaves. We don't have one."

"It's all right. *I* know."

"I'll have bacon and tomato, too," Melissa said. "What's your name again? I forgot."

"Darcy," I said.

Shana echoed it. "Darcy. I want jelly butter."

"She means peanut butter and jelly," Melissa translated.

Jeremy got up on a chair and got down a big yellow plastic platter. He started spreading a thick layer of paper towels on it and then separating the slices of bacon to put on the towels. He seemed to know what he was doing, so I went ahead and made the sandwich for Shana.

"How long, Jeremy?" Melissa asked, opening the microwave oven for the platter of a whole pound of bacon, which had now been covered over with more paper towels.

"You fix the bread and then I'll cut the tomatoes while the bacon cooks," Jeremy said authoritatively. "I'll set the timer."

The door was closed, the controls punched, and the light came on inside. I guessed he was handling it all right when, after a minute or two, the aroma of bacon drifted through the room.

I helped Melissa put mayonnaise on the bread, talked them into lettuce along with the tomatoes, and was feeling reasonably in control when the timer went off on the oven.

"Oh, crumb! I must've done something wrong,"

Jeremy said, peering inside the microwave. "Maybe I set it for too many minutes."

I moved along the counter to look inside, and my stomach twisted.

The bacon had cooked, all right, the slices around the edges being charred almost black. That wasn't the worst of it, though. As the bacon cooked, the grease had melted out of it, and the yellow platter wasn't deep enough to hold it all. The grease ran in a great yellowish puddle down over the floor of the oven, onto the counter, and it didn't take long to see why it had such a peculiar color.

The plastic platter had split and blistered and melted, so that it mingled with the liquid bacon fat in a lake that threatened to overflow onto the floor.

Luckily there were paper towels in sight, which I grabbed and began mopping up the mess. I remembered, now, something about needing special dishes to cook in a microwave. Not plastic ones, I guessed.

Jeremy looked disappointedly at the bacon. "I think it's all burned up."

"No, the slices in the middle are all right.

You like it crisp, don't you? There's enough for two sandwiches, one for you and one for Melissa." I picked out the salvageable bacon and scooped up the rest of the mess to put it into the garbage can under the sink. I hoped the platter wasn't anybody's favorite and that I wouldn't be blamed for allowing Jeremy to use it in the oven. What a way to get started on a new job!

They ate at a picnic table in the back yard, and I left them there when a bell sounded within the house. "The doorbell?" I asked, and the other kids nodded, their mouths too full to reply.

I'd reached the front door when it occurred to me that even though it was broad daylight, it might not be wise to allow anyone into the house.

There was no window in the door, so I couldn't see out. "Who is it?" I called.

A man's voice answered. "Gas company. I'm here to check the gas lines."

I hesitated. I'd feel like a fool if I didn't let him in and the Fosters thought I should have. Yet I'd heard so many times about criminals misrepresenting themselves as service men, and I knew there were plenty of valuables in this house for a crook to steal.

"I'm sorry," I said finally. "I'm the baby-sitter, and I'm not authorized to let anyone in."

"I'm from the gas company," the man said, sounding impatient. "There's a problem with the gas lines in this neighborhood, and I need to get inside to check them. I have identification. Open the door, and I'll show it to you."

I hesitated again. What if there really was a problem? Something dangerous? Would the house blow up if I didn't let him inside?

"Go over to the window, to the left of the door," I decided. "You can show me the ID through the window." I didn't know what else to do.

I heard him swear softly, and then, as I walked toward the nearest window, still feeling uneasy about the whole thing, I heard his boots on the tiles. There were decorative wrought iron bars over the windows, on the outside, so he couldn't get the wallet right close to the glass, and it was very shadowy out there. He was wearing a blue coverall, all right, but though I craned my neck, I couldn't see any gas company van on the street. And I couldn't read what was written on the plastic card he held up, either.

"Look, I'm in a hurry," the man said, his voice muffled. He was tall and slim, that was all I could tell. I couldn't get any better look at his face than at his ID.

I was feeling more and more uncertain and foolish, but something held me back from opening the door to him. I kept remembering those boring lectures Mrs. Hopkins gave at school, mostly intended for latch-key kids who spent a lot of time at home by themselves.

"I'm sorry," I said. "I can't let you in. If it's really an emergency, have the police come here with you. There's a patrol through this area every day. Just have them send a patrol car. When I see that, I'll open the door."

Again the man swore, and a minute later I could see, peering through the barred window and out through one of the white plastered arches, the man in blue coveralls striding away toward the street.

No doubt everybody would laugh at me for

being so silly, I thought, checking to make sure the front door was locked the way Mrs. Murphy had left it.

I went back through the house to the kitchen. Through the window I saw the Foster kids throwing their bread crusts at each other, laughing as a smear of mayonnaise left a trail across Melissa's nose. It was a good thing I'd had them eat outdoors. I looked at the clock.

Only two and a half hours to go before the housekeeper came home, I thought, and hoped nothing else unexpected would happen.

Chapter Four

The trouble with watching three kids at once is that they can go in three different directions, and you can only go in one.

While the kids were all playing outside, I sat in a plastic chair and watched them scattered over the lawn. The pool was there, behind a high chain-link fence; fortunately, the kids couldn't get at it. I didn't have a bathing suit, and I wasn't sure enough yet of the kids to know I could keep up with all three of them in the water.

Shana saw me looking at the pool and leaned against my knee. "I can swim," she told me.

"She's not supposed to go in the deep end, though," Melissa said. "Can you read, Darcy?"

"Yes, of course I can read. Can you?"

She shook her dark head, and the soft

little curls danced around her face. "No. I won't go to kindergarten until next year. Jeremy can read *some,* but not whole books. Will you read us a story?"

I felt safe reading stories, I did that all the time; so we went inside and sat in the play-room. They had more books than the library, and they each chose one and sat beside me on the big squashy couch.

"Mine first," Shana insisted, thrusting a book into my hands. *"Greg-ry Gray and the Brave Beast."* It was about a little red-headed boy who was left to spend his vacation alone with the housekeeper in a big old Victorian house, while all the other boys in the school went home to their families; Gregory made friends with a big, tough alley cat called Lionel. Obviously the kids knew it by heart. If I left out a word, they filled it in, in a chorus.

I read until my throat got dry. "I need a drink," I said, and then I realized that only Melissa and Jeremy were sitting beside me. "Where's Shana?"

"Maybe she's tired," Melissa suggested. "Sometimes she takes a nap."

The little girl wasn't in her bedroom though. She didn't answer when we called her name, so I went looking through the house. It occurred to me that the gas man hadn't come back, nor had the police come to say it was truly an emergency. Maybe they'd discovered whatever the problem was, somewhere else, and they hadn't needed to come back. I looked into the master bedroom.

And there she was.

Shana was seated at the dressing table, intent on her own small face in the mirror before her. Lipstick was smeared across the lower part of her face, and she was trying to apply eye shadow with ludicrous results.

"Oh, Shanny, shame on you!" Melissa cried, and the applicator jumped in Shana's hand, leaving a blue mark across one cheekbone.

"Like Mama," Shana said, unrepentant, as I took the applicator out of her hand.

"You can do this when you get bigger," I said, seeing no damage that soap and water wouldn't take care of, except for the gouge in the cake of eye shadow. I wondered how Mrs. Murphy managed to keep up with all three of them at once."

I guess I must have asked the question aloud, because Melissa piped up the answer. "She keeps the doors locked so we can't get in."

"In all the rooms? This one, and your father's study, and your mother's?"

Melissa nodded solemnly. "And the door to the basement, after Jeremy broke his arm falling off the back swing."

Wonderful, I thought sourly. Why hadn't the housekeeper locked those rooms for my benefit? I lifted Shana down from the stool and headed for the bathroom, then changed my mind about using *that* bathroom. Better to use the one the girls shared.

Melissa trotted beside me. "She unlocks the doors before Mama gets home," she offered.

Oh-ho. Mrs./Dr. Foster didn't know some of the rooms were kept tidy because the children weren't allowed to get into them. I wasn't sure if this was fair or not. Sensible, probably; but if it was all above-board, why keep it a secret from the lady of the house? I figured it *was* a secret, or the housekeeper wouldn't unlock the doors before Mrs./Dr. Foster came home.

"Does Mrs. Murphy live here, in this house?"

I asked as I chose a brown washcloth to get the goop off Shana's face. She felt soft to my touch, and she didn't object to being washed.

"She has a room downstairs," Melissa said, nodding. "Sometimes she goes to see her son Kenneth, but she doesn't like Kenneth's wife, so it's not very often."

I finished with Shana and looked around. "Where's Jeremy?"

This time we found the missing one easily. He was in his father's study, talking on the telephone. He looked up and smiled at us, speaking into the phone. "All right. Good-bye, Uncle Rick." He hung up and informed me, "I was talking to my uncle. He lives in Hawaii."

I hadn't heard the phone ring. "Did you call him, or did he call you?"

"I called him," Jeremy said importantly. "This number, right here." He leaned forward over an open directory, holding a finger near the numbers written after the last name. "It's easy, you just punch the button for each number, and if it's a long one like this, you have to punch *one* first."

What did it cost to call Hawaii? Day rates?

I swallowed. "I don't think you'd better call any more, unless Mrs. Murphy says you can."

"She won't let me call," Jeremy said, smiling. "Where's Melissa?"

That was the way it went. I only had two arms; I couldn't keep hold of all three of them at once, and if I knew where two of them were, the third disappeared. Nothing else horrible happened, but I was sure glad when Mrs. Murphy came home.

"Did it hurt?" I asked sympathetically. I never had a root canal, and Mom says if I go every six months for checkups and brush and floss between times, I probably never will. But it made me feel peculiar, thinking about it.

"Oh, Dr. Hughes is a very good dentist," the housekeeper said. "I was nervous and tense. But it wasn't too terrible. How did things go here?"

I hesitated. "Well, Shana got into her mother's makeup, but it all washed off. And a platter melted in the microwave. I had to throw it in the garbage can. A yellow plastic platter." I held my breath, waiting to hear that it was somebody's favorite one.

"Jeremy cooking in the microwave again? Last time he heated rolls without wrapping them in a napkin first, and they came out hard enough to be bullets." She sighed. "You'll have to be careful, or they'll talk you into things."

I wanted to ask what things; how was I supposed to know what they were allowed, or not allowed, to do? She didn't give me a chance, though. She was heading for the kitchen.

"Time to put the roast on, they're having company tonight. Then I think I'll rest a bit, in my room."

"Do you dare lie down when they're playing?" I asked.

"Oh, yes, they'll stay outside," she said, and I wondered if she locked them outdoors as well as out of some of the rooms.

"There was a gas man here," I said hesitantly, standing in the kitchen doorway. "He wanted in, but I couldn't see his ID, so I told him I couldn't open the door."

She was tying on an apron. "Oh? Well, if it's important, he'll be back, no doubt. My next appointment is day after tomorrow, same time. You'll be here at one again then?"

"Sure," I agreed. "Good-bye until then."

Melissa hung onto my hand, walking me to the front door. "I like you for a sitter," she told me, and I squeezed back on her hand.

"Oh. I forgot to tell Mrs. Murphy that Jeremy called his uncle in Hawaii." I wondered if I should go back.

"Oh, Daddy will know when the bill comes," Melissa said. "He always says, 'That kid's been calling long distance again,' and Mama tells Jeremy not to do it anymore. Next time," she said, quite complacently, "he's going to call Grandma Foster. She lives in Texas. She has a dog. Mama won't let us have a dog. Our other grandma lives in Seattle. She has three cats. We called her last week."

"How do you know the numbers?" I asked. Jeremy surely couldn't read very well, at six years old.

"Oh, Jeremy has them marked in Daddy's book. He watched when Daddy called each of them, and then he made a secret code sign by the name, so he knows which number belongs to which person. Uncle Rick's sign is like this." She marked an invisible X in the air.

Well, if *they* couldn't keep Jeremy from calling people all over the world, I didn't see how they'd expect me to do it. "I'll see you again day after tomorrow," I told her, and let myself out the front door.

I rode home, not sure how well it had gone. At least nobody'd gotten hurt. I couldn't judge how serious the Fosters would consider the damage of the platter or the eye shadow. But though it was a relief to have the first day over, I wasn't too apprehensive about the next time I would stay with the kids.

Irene was sitting in our kitchen when I got home, watching my mom stuff a pair of chickens for roasting. I helped myself to a banana to match the one Irene was eating, and said, "The little one says 'shicken' and you have to figure out if she means chicken or kitchen."

Mom started to truss up the first bird with dental floss, the way she usually did, giving me a smile. "How was it?"

I sank into a chair beside Irene. "Okay, I guess. Those kids have everything to play with you ever heard of. Including a neat dollhouse, Irene. Remember how we used to play with that old one of mine? Of course we're too big for that stuff now, but I still kind of like to look at them. Maybe they wouldn't care if I took you in and showed you the place."

Mom gave me a look. "No visitors while you're on the job unless you have permission, Darcy."

"Yeah, I know. Come on, Irene, let's go jog around the park or something. I need some exercise."

I didn't ask her why she was here before I got home, when she knew I'd be at the Fosters until four o'clock. Tim and a couple of buddies were working on the Volks in the driveway, and she'd needed an excuse to walk past them and say, "Hi, Tim." I knew how he'd answered: a grunted "Hi" without even pulling his head out from under the hood. Irene never gave up, though.

"When he's twenty-one," she said once, "I'll be seventeen. Then I'll be old enough for him, don't you think?"

"When he's twenty-one, he'll probably be gone, at the police academy," I told her. "That's all he thinks about, becoming a cop. It'll take a couple of years at the junior college, and then the academy, and he might go away somewhere to get a job."

"I'll bet he'll look darling in a police uniform," Irene said. Trust her to see the positive side of everything.

We went past the boys, who had paused for cold drinks. Irene said "Hi, Tim," and he lifted a lazy hand to wave without speaking. As long as we were where they could see us, Irene walked in that special way she saves for such times. After that, she broke into a trot beside me, heading toward the park.

There were a few mothers with small children there, near the wading pool and the playground equipment. We cut off in the opposite direction—I'd had enough of small children for one day. The park is a nice one, with lots of open space plus some woods and little ravines.

We ran across the grass to get onto a path, where I took the lead and kept going until I got tired. Puffing, I flopped down on the grassy hillside, and Irene stretched out flat beside me.

It didn't take her long to get her wind back, though, and she sat up, staring down into the ravine to where a small waterwheel turned on the stream.

"What's that?"

"What?" I asked, following her gaze.

"It looks like a tent. You can't camp in the park, can you?"

I squinted to see better. "I think it's just a sheet of plastic. It probably blew down there."

"It looks more like somebody fastened it over those bushes to make a shelter."

I shrugged. "Kids playing. We used to make tents out of blankets over card tables or clotheslines, or tied between trees."

Irene shoved herself to her feet. "I'm going down and look."

At first I thought I'd just sit there and watch her, but then I decided, what the heck, I might as well tag along. I didn't expect to find anything, though.

She *was* right about somebody making a shelter, though I still thought it was just kids. The sheet of dark plastic was almost the same color as the shrubs, so it didn't show up from very far away, and the grass was beaten down beneath it, as if someone had been sitting or lying there.

"Look," Irene said. She was down on her hands and knees, groping around, coming up with an old sweatshirt and an empty box that had held crackers.

"Playing house is always more fun if you have something real to eat," I said, remembering. "This is fairly cozy, isn't it? Bushes on three sides so it's almost like walls. Bobby and Jimmy would like it."

Irene sat down, holding up the sweatshirt. "This isn't kid size. I think someone's hiding here, Darce."

Sometimes a grunt like Tim makes is as good a way as any to answer Irene. You can't talk her out of ideas, so you just wait until they wear off.

"Hey, look! There's a book!"

It was a paperback, well-worn and dog-eared. I remembered it from school; it was one our class got from a book club for free reading time. "I read this. It's about a girl who's abused by her mother. Isn't it one of the ones Miss

Stanton said was missing from our homeroom bookshelf?"

We were sitting there staring at each other, thinking it out and not saying anything, when we heard rustling in the bushes outside. And then a head popped through the opening at the end of the plastic tarp shelter.

chapter five

For a few seconds Diana Hazen's surprised face stared at us, and then she yelped and scrambled backward on her hands and knees. She wasn't fast enough, though. Irene reached out and grabbed her wrist, and they struggled silently, until Diana suddenly collapsed on the ground and started to cry.

"Hey! Diana, don't cry! We won't tell anybody where you are, will we, Darce?"

I hadn't decided on my answer to that when Diana lifted a wet face and studied us.

Diana would have been pretty if she hadn't been so skinny, and if somebody'd told her what to do with her hair. She had red hair, too, but it was the frizzy kind, and she let it grow too long, so it stuck out sort of like a brush pile around her face.

She had very fair skin with more freckles than I have and eyes that were pale blue. She pushed herself into a sitting position and wiped her eyes with the backs of her hands. "How'd you find me?"

"We saw the plastic and figured some kids built a shelter. We were just checking it out. How long have you been here?" Irene asked.

Diana inhaled deeply. "Two days."

"We met a cop yesterday," I told her. "He was asking about you, if we'd seen you."

"What did you tell him?" There was a stubborn defiance in the delicate face.

"Told him we didn't know where you were, of course," Irene said, and I added, "And that you'd probably run away again because you weren't treated very well at home. That's true, isn't it?"

It was crowded in the little hiding place. Diana looked around and reached for the paperback book and the sweatshirt, then held them as if she didn't know what to do next. "Are you going to turn me in?"

"We said we wouldn't rat on you," Irene said. "We told the cop it wasn't your fault you ran away, that you had to because your dad hits you. Why don't you talk to him? I'll bet he'd investigate."

Diana didn't have a handkerchief, so she sniffed. "It wouldn't do any good. The police talked to me before, and they called the protective services, but my dad told them I lied, that I was incorrigible, and he only hit me when I sassed him back."

"He leaves bruises on you," I said, imagining what that would be like, glad *my* dad never touched me except to give me a hug once in a while. "If they saw the bruises—"

"He says I get hurt by being clumsy, running into things, falling down."

Irene's mouth was slightly open. "You mean they believe him, even when you tell them he hits you?"

Diana spoke very softly. "I don't tell them. It doesn't do any good. He used to hit my sister Ellen, too; and when she tried to tell anybody, he just beat her up after they left. I'm not old enough to get married, the way Ellen did; but my brother George is getting out of boot camp in three weeks. He says when he does, he'll pay my bus fare out to where he is, in San Diego. My aunt lives there, and she'll take me in if George can help pay my bus fare. Until then, I have to hide out."

We sat for a minute in silence, appalled, knowing she wasn't being dramatic. She didn't have to say what her dad would do if he found her; we'd seen the black-and-blue marks before. There was a bruise on her cheek now, turning greenish yellow.

"You can't stay here," Irene said after a while, sounding strangled. "They'll find you when they cut the grass, even if they don't notice you before that."

"They mowed it day before yesterday," Diana said. "They won't cut it again until next week. I'll go somewhere else while they do it."

"Where?" I asked, sounding hollow, the way I felt.

"I don't know. I'll think of something."

Irene cleared her throat. "Have you got any money? To buy food with?"

"Three dollars and six cents," Diana said.

To last three weeks? I thought, I remembered the chickens my mom was roasting, and all the other stuff that would go with it.

"I had some crackers," she told us, indicating the empty box. "I ate the last of them last night, though."

"And you haven't had anything to eat today?" There was horror in Irene's tone.

No wonder Diana was skinny. My mind was racing. I knew my folks would expect me to cooperate with the police, but I also knew I couldn't turn Diana in, even if Irene hadn't promised for both of us.

"Darcy, you have any money?" Irene demanded, digging into her jeans' pocket. "I've got eighty-two cents. Here."

Diana just looked at the coins. "I can't take your money."

"Don't be silly. I'll get my allowance again on Friday night, and I don't have to depend on it to eat. We'll get you some food, won't we, Darcy?" She reached over and dropped the money into the pocket of the sweatshirt.

"I don't have any cash, not until Mrs. Foster

pays me for baby-sitting," I had to admit. "I can get some food, though."

A touch of interest showed in Diana's face. "You baby-sitting for the Fosters? The ones on Oakwood Drive?"

"Yes. You know them?"

"My sister Ellen used to sit for them once in a while." A little of the tension went out of her, talking about something other than her own predicament. "She said they were horrid. The boy painted the baby bright blue one day. It was water-base paint, but even so she had an awful time getting it off. Ellen thought they shouldn't have left the paint where the kids could get it, but Mr. Foster was more upset about cleaning up the garage than getting the color out of the baby's hair."

"Neat kids," Irene said, and giggled.

A small smile curled the ends of Diana's mouth, and I realized how seldom I'd seen her smile. She was pretty. "Ellen was only there a couple of times, then she got a full-time job at Burger King, but she'd tell me the things those kids did."

I told them the things that had happened while I was there, and they laughed. I could tell they were glad they hadn't been the baby-sitters, though.

"The worst thing," Diana said, "was the last day Ellen was there. Jeremy built a bonfire and scorched the side of the house. She wasn't watching him because Melissa had tried to shampoo Shana's hair and got soap in her eyes, and they were both screaming bloody murder. Shana's eyes hurt, and Melissa was afraid she'd blinded her."

"You can't watch all three of them at the same time," I admitted uneasily. "I've never been fired from a sitting job, but maybe this will be the first time."

"I went there once, while Ellen was working there," Diana said. "It sure is a nice house. All those soft carpets and big comfortable chairs and things. My dad wouldn't hardly believe me when I told him about two big freezers full of food. And seven televisions, all color!" There was wonder in her voice.

I moved uncomfortably. "I'm getting a cramp from crouching here this way. And I think it's time I went home for supper. I'll bring you back something to eat, Diana. And maybe a blanket. I think there's an old one in the hall closet that nobody will miss—"

"Me, too," Irene added. "We'll see you later, Diana."

We left her there, clutching the old sweatshirt that must have served as blanket or pillow, whichever she needed the most, and that tattered book about an abused child.

My throat ached, thinking about her. Irene was babbling along for a minute or so before I realized what she was saying. "—your garage?"

"What? What are you talking about?"

"I said, isn't there a room over your garage? Where she could hide and be safer than where she is?"

"With Tim and all those guys in and out every few minutes, getting tools? He's making his spending money this summer cutting grass, with our mower, so he's in and out for that, too."

I felt rotten about it, but I had to say it. "Irene, maybe the best thing for Diana would be to tell somebody about her. My mom would know what was the best thing to do—"

"Dance, you promised! You promised not to tell!"

"No, I didn't. You promised for both of us," I objected.

"Well, you didn't say you didn't promise, when I said it. That's the same as saying it yourself. My gosh, Darcy, imagine what it must be like for her at home. She only has to stay hidden for three weeks, and then her brother will get her away from here. Once she's in San Diego she'll be okay. We *have* to help her!"

"I know we have to help. I'm just not sure that feeding her and not telling anybody about her is the way to do it. That young cop we met, that Chris Roberts, I *know* he'd try to get some help for her—"

"You heard what she said. Her sister told, and they couldn't help *her.* If your dad mistreated you, would you dare stand there in front of him and tell people what he did, unless you were *positive* they'd take you away immediately and protect you from him?"

I had to confess I wouldn't. "Our garage isn't a good place, though. There's nothing but junk in that room, and nowhere for her to sleep that's any better than where she is, really. And no way to get her in and out. There are too many people around our garage, and no telling when Jimmy and Bobby will decide to go upstairs for something. One summer the neighborhood kids used it as a club house."

"What about that tree house they had last year? Do they still play in it?"

My steps slowed. "That might be an idea. I don't think they've been in it since Jimmy fell out of it and broke his arm last August. Dad got sort of annoyed about it, and they lost interest. It's on the other side of the house from the garage, too, in the edge of the woods. I'll check it out when I get home."

I still felt as if I ought to discuss it with my folks, or at least with Tim. For a brother, Tim wasn't bad, and he knew how cops thought about things. He and Clancy were good friends, and sometimes he rode on patrol with Clancy.

I couldn't quite bring myself to give Diana away, though. It was true that when I hadn't protested what Irene said, I was sort of giving a promise of my own.

I felt guilty, eating roasted chicken and

potatoes and gravy and buttered corn and salad and spice cake, thinking about Diana and the empty box of crackers. Even if she had a few dollars, she didn't dare go any place where she'd be recognized to buy anything, and I went to the store for Mom often enough to know how little you could get for three or four dollars.

Mom had a meeting that evening, and Dad was helping Tim overhaul an engine, out in the garage. I washed the dishes and left them draining dry, then started checking to see what I could take to Diana.

There were two chicken legs and a thigh left, not enough to go around again or put into a casserole, I decided. I stuck them in a plastic sandwich bag and probed further. There were leftover mashed potatoes, but I didn't think they'd transport well, nor taste good cold, though Diana probably wasn't particular. Salad, though—with a plastic fork to eat it— and some bread and butter. On impulse, I buttered six slices and packaged them and took some cheese and lunch meat, then one each of the apples, oranges, and bananas from the bowl in the middle of the table. I put all this in a paper bag, stashed it on the front porch, and went out to see how the tree house looked.

It had been there ever since I could remember. Tim and Dad built it together when Tim was younger than Bobby was now. I'd played in it too, when I was a little kid.

The ladder up to it—boards nailed up the side of the tree—still seemed sturdy enough. I looked inside and saw only a few dead leaves and a spider.

It was big enough for a person to lie down comfortably, it had a roof and two windows and an open doorway, and this time of year it was almost hidden in foliage.

Irene was right. It was an ideal place for Diana.

By the time I had it ready for her, it was dusk. I walked back through the summer evening to the park, checking to make sure nobody was paying any attention to me before I strolled down into the ravine.

Irene was there ahead of me, and we laughed as we compared the supplies we'd brought. Irene had three chocolate bars, a cold pork chop, two peanut butter and jelly sandwiches, two cans of diet pop, and a bag of sunflower seeds.

Diana ate the sandwiches and the pork chop and two pieces of fruit so quickly that Irene and I looked at each other and swallowed hard. Neither of us had ever been *really* hungry, not as hungry as Diana was.

I told her about the tree house. "You'll have to go there after it's full dark," I told her. "I don't dare stay here with you until then. My folks get excited if I'm not home before dark, and I don't want them calling the police. Just go along the hedge on the east side of the house, and there'll be enough light from the downstairs bathroom so you can find the tree. I put a blanket and pillow up there, and an air mattress."

Diana's blue eyes filled with moisture. "I don't know how to thank you," she said.

I nearly cried myself. I hoped I was doing the right thing and that my folks would understand when they found out about it.

I ran most of the way home, and when I got there the boys and Dad were still out in the garage and hadn't noticed I'd been gone.

I got ready for bed and was reading when Tim came upstairs. "Tim. Are you alone?" I called out.

He paused in my doorway, not touching anything because he had grease all over his hands and shirt front. "No, I have a princess with me, waiting for me to take her to the ball. She'll turn into a pumpkin at midnight, so I have to hurry."

"I think it was the coach that turned into a pumpkin," I said. "Listen, can I ask you a legal question? In confidence?"

He checked his shoulder to make sure it was clean, then slouched against the door-frame. "Sure. Are the cops after you for jay walking, or what?"

I didn't smile. "It's a hypothetical case. Suppose somebody runs away from home, someone under age, I mean. And her folks call the cops. What will they do if they pick her up?"

"You thinking about running away?" His blue eyes sharpened. His red hair was almost like Diana's, except that he kept it cut short so it could just barely curl.

"I said hypothetical. What would they do?"

"Take her home, I guess. Why?"

"Even if they knew she was mistreated at home?"

He looked at me, then stepped inside the room and pulled up a chair beside my bed. "If she said she was mistreated, I suppose they'd call the Child Protective Agency, and they'd send somebody out to investigate."

"And in the meantime? Would they make her go home?"

He considered this. "They might. Depending on whether they believed her or not. Does she have bruises? Burns? Hypothetically speaking, of course?"

"Not right now, except for a bruise that's almost gone. They wouldn't put her in a foster home or anything like that, if her folks said she was lying?"

"It would probably be up to a judge to decide. I'm not sure. You want me to ask Clancy?"

I thought about it, then slowly shook my head. "No. Maybe you better not." Clancy would know who I meant. He'd know they were supposed to be looking for Diana and that she was my age. He couldn't fail to figure it out, and I didn't want Clancy to ask me any questions I didn't care to answer. "Do they call out the FBI for runaways?"

"Not unless there's some reason to think someone has taken them across state lines," Tim said promptly. "Like in a kidnapping. Lots of places, they don't even look very hard for runaways, unless they're little kids. How old is this hypothetical runaway? Thirteen, maybe?"

I flushed, but held my ground. "About, I guess. Listen, what if someone else helps a runaway? Is it a criminal offense?"

Tim thoughtfully ran a thumb over his chin and left a black smear. "You sure you want to keep this hypothetical, Darcy?"

"I have to."

"Okay. Well, as far as I know, if the runaway isn't a criminal, then you can't be accused of being an accessory to anything. Mom and Dad might be upset with you, though, if you're helping someone hide out."

I didn't argue about that. "If you have to feel guilty no matter what you do, you might as well follow your own conscience, I guess," I muttered.

Tim was still looking thoughtful. He stood up when he heard the younger boys on the stairs. "I have to get in the bathroom before the beasts take it over. I hope you know what you're doing, Darce."

I hoped so, too. For a little while I forgot all about the Foster kids and my responsibilities for them.

Chapter Six

Between worrying about harboring a fugitive in our tree house and wondering what Jeremy Foster would do to get me fired from my baby-sitting job, I was a wreck. I'd kept secrets from my mom before, silly things like walking past Ted Hansen's house so he'd see me and say "Hi," or eating two Hershey bars at Irene's in one afternoon. I'd never concealed anything serious from her, though, and it bothered me.

For one thing, I wasn't at all sure that hiding Diana was the best thing to do, not even for her own sake. I'd have liked my mother's advice on that—she'd have cared about another kid enough to make the effort to get the kind of help Diana needed. Most of the time I felt quite grown up, but some things take more than thirteen years of experience, and this seemed like one of them. Yet the secret wasn't really mine to share.

And I dreamed about the Foster kids. The thing Diana told us about Jeremy building a fire that scorched the wall of the house was scary, and in my dream he burned down the whole house. It was so vivid in my mind, the flames leaping and the fire engines screaming to the rescue, that I woke up gasping and had trouble going back to sleep.

I *did* tell Mom about the dream. She didn't laugh, as I half expected her to do.

"He really did build a fire?"

"That's what—" I almost said Diana's name, and quickly remembered to change it, in case they listed runaway kids in the paper or gave their names on TV or something. "This girl told me. Her sister sat them a few times, and Jeremy built a fire. Some of the other things he does aren't dangerous, just messy or annoying, but the idea of a fire scares me."

"And most of the time this Mrs. Murphy, the housekeeper, is the one who takes care of them? I wonder how much time they spend with their parents."

"I don't know. Mr. Foster is president of a big bank, and Mrs./Dr. Foster is a psychiatrist. Irene says she has an office in the Garden Park Building. They're gone all day, both of them. Mrs. Murphy keeps the kids from messing up some of the rooms by locking the kids out of them, and I've got a hunch that when she wants a nap she locks them out of the whole house, in the back yard. It's got a high fence around it; they can't get out, but still . . ."

Mom nodded. "Still, that's not the way to look after small children. It makes me wonder if the kids aren't doing some rather outrageous things just to make someone pay attention to them. That business about calling their grandmothers, in Seattle and Texas, it's the kind of thing I'd expect when they need affection from someone. It doesn't sound as if their parents are around enough, and the housekeeper might not do any more than look after their physical needs—keep them clean and fed, I mean. Children need more than that."

I thought guiltily of my own approach to the Foster kids—all I had to do was keep them from killing each other, I'd thought. "You had more kids than the Fosters," I said. "How did you keep track of all of us?"

She laughed. "Well, I wasn't working part time then; I was home with you until after you started school. Tim was good at watching over you younger ones, but I didn't depend on him to do it all. We read together and played games and talked a lot, and you knew what was expected of you. Your dad and I were consistent in what we asked of you, and we always spent time together as a family. Remember the fun we had when you were little, going camping and on picnics? I wonder if the Fosters do things like that with their kids? That reminds me, Dad is getting things together for his camping trip with the boys this weekend, and he can't find his air mattress. It didn't get put away in your closet somehow, did it?"

Another thing to feel guilty about, I thought wildly. "No, uh, I'm sure it's not in my closet," I said, hoping I sounded calm. I wasn't used to this kind of thing, and I wouldn't have been surprised if my thoughts had been plain to see in my face. I never even thought about the upcoming camping trip when I fixed up the tree house for Diana.

"I guess he can take mine," Mom said, returning her attention to the casseroles she was making to put in the freezer. She did that on days she wasn't working so when she got busy we could just defrost something to eat. "Since I'm not going this time. I guess I'm getting too busy, too. I miss the things we used to do together. Maybe the next time they camp out, you and I should go, too. What do you think?"

"Okay," I agreed. "Mom, what do you think I should do about the Foster kids? It's hard to find something fascinating to do that will interest all three of them at once."

"I don't know what to tell you, Darcy. Except that if you show them you like them, they'll probably behave for you."

"Jeremy may be hard to like," I said slowly.

"That means he needs liking, or loving, most of all, I suspect. Children will sometimes push a parent with unacceptable behavior, until the parent sets a limit to it. Tim was terrible that way, but when we told him he simply could not do certain things, and then stopped him from doing them, he seemed relieved that it had all been settled, and he stopped fighting us on that issue. Until the next issue came along, of course."

My mom didn't have a degree in psychology, but she seemed pretty smart to me. "I don't understand why Mrs./Dr. Foster doesn't know what's happening with her own kids, though," I said. "She's a psychiatrist, for pete's sake."

Mom fastened foil over the tops of the casserole dishes and sealed them shut. "Here, put these in the freezer for me, will you? The thing is, Darcy, it's a lot easier to look at other people's children and see what's wrong with them than to interpret what's happening right under your nose. We're too close to our own families and it's easier to pretend nothing's wrong than to have to try to deal with the problems. Maybe I'm mistaken about the Foster kids, but it can't hurt to be firm but loving with them. I never saw a child who didn't respond to love."

So I went to work the next day determined to love Jeremy if it killed me, and that lasted for about twenty minutes after Mrs. Murphy had gone off to her dental appointment.

We started off all right. They'd had lunch, this time, so we didn't have to risk cooking anything. Shana wanted a story—the same one, *Gregory Gray and the Brave Beast*—so I read that while the other kids were looking for books.

"She always wants that one," Melissa told me. "It's her favorite."

By the time I finished the first story, Melissa was there with her book, but Jeremy had disappeared.

"Just a minute," I told the girls, "I have to find Jeremy."

And right then this horrible noise began, so that my hair stood on end and chills ran all through me. It was loud and terrifying and made me want to scream at it to stop.

It didn't stop, though. It would break off for a few seconds, and then start again. "What is it?" I asked wildly, looking around for the source of the sound.

Shana sat on the couch, her book closed on her lap, blue eyes very wide and startled. Melissa held her hands over her ears and scrunched up her face.

"It's the burglar alarm, I think," Melissa said.

Burglars? In the middle of the afternoon?

The racket was awesome; I felt as if I were being assaulted, and I didn't know what to do. Call the police? I looked around for the tele-phone.

Jeremy suddenly appeared in the doorway of the playroom, looking about the way I felt—frightened.

"What did you do, Jeremy?" Melissa asked, and he shook his head.

"I didn't do anything," he protested ear-nestly, "honest I didn't."

It was hard to recover my wits with that alarm going off. I didn't know much about bur-glar alarms, but there must be a way to turn it off. I asked Jeremy.

"I don't know. Is there really a burglar?"

"I don't know," I echoed. "I think we'd better call the police. Where's the telephone?"

It was hard to think, to dial, even with the number written on a sticker on the phone book so I didn't have to look it up. If I were the burglar, I thought, if there *was* a burglar, I'd run for my life, with that sound going on and on. It must be almost loud enough to be heard over at our house.

In a moment, between the blasts of the alarm, I heard two separate sounds. Someone pounding on the front door and a siren.

"Marysville Police Department," a voice said in my ear.

"Uh, I'm the baby-sitter at the Foster home on Oakwood Drive," I said nervously. "Ah—" I had to wait for the next blast of sound to end before I could continue. "The burglar alarm is going off, and I don't know why, or how to stop it—"

"We have an officer on the way," the dispatcher's voice said calmly. I suppose it was easier to stay calm when you weren't where the crime was actually taking place.

Jeremy ran to the front of the house to peer through the windows, which were covered with the iron grillwork. I had thought that was decorative, but now I wondered if the windows were barred to keep burglars out. They were all that way except the ones that opened inside the fenced yard.

Could someone really have attempted to burglarize the house? Or had Jeremy, in spite of his denial, been responsible for setting off the alarm?

"The cops are here!" Jeremy said excitedly as I entered the front hallway.

He struggled with the lock and opened the door as a police car pulled in at the curb, closely followed by a second patrol unit. Jeremy ran out to meet them, shouting, "It's a burglar! It's a burglar!"

I had a fleeting memory of my mother saying kids sometimes did things to get attention; and then two of the officers were entering the house. One of them, I was both glad and embarrassed to see, was Tim's friend Clancy.

Clancy was about my father's age and had a magnificent handlebar mustache like someone out of an old movie. He looked at me and then at Jeremy, who was jiggling up and down, hopping from one foot to the other.

"Hello, Darcy. What happened here?"

"I don't know. Just all of a sudden that horrible alarm went off. I didn't see anything," I said.

"You see anything, son? Any person looking in a window, anything like that?"

Jeremy stopped jumping; his brown eyes were shining, though. "No. I didn't see anything. But it's a burglar, isn't it? The alarm went off!"

"I'll check around the back," one of the younger officers said, and disappeared. Another one started through the house, and a minute later the alarm stopped. The quiet was almost as unnatural, at first, as the noise had been.

"Where were you when it went off, Jeremy?" I asked. I could usually tell by looking at my younger brothers if they were telling the truth or not, but I didn't know Jeremy very well yet.

"In my room, looking for my *Star Wars* book. All of a sudden it went off. It made my hair prick," he said, and touched the back of his neck.

That made me kind of inclined to believe him, because that was how it affected me, too.

"Do you think the burglar got any of Mama's jewelry?" Melissa asked, leaning into my side.

Clancy squatted down so he was more on a level with her. "Where does your mama keep her jewelry? Do you know?"

"In a box in the bedroom. It's in the wall," Melissa said.

"It's not a box, it's a safe," Jeremy corrected her. "There's one in Daddy's study, too, but it just has papers in it, or maybe money. I can show you," he offered.

I went with them to look at both wall safes. Clancy made a grunting sound, and I finally realized where Tim got his habit of making that sound instead of using words.

"Nobody's been at either of them," Clancy said. "You hear anything, Darcy, before the alarm went off?"

"No. I didn't notice anything."

"All the kids with you when it began?"

"No. Jeremy was in his room, looking for a book."

"You try to open a window or anything like that, son?"

Jeremy shook his head. "No. Daddy says we're not supposed to open the windows, or it will set off the alarm. Besides, the air conditioner doesn't work right if the windows are open."

I was beginning to feel wobbly in the middle. What if Jeremy hadn't done anything to set off the alarm? What if there had been a burglar? What if there hadn't been an alarm, and someone had gotten into the house?

About that time, as we walked back toward the entry hall, a young officer came back. "Looks like somebody tried to jimmy the lock on the side door into the garage," he said.

The feeling in my stomach got worse.

"It's a blind area, big high hedge shields that side of the house from the neighbors. They didn't see anything, though they looked out when the alarm went off. Doug's checking out the alley, to see if anybody went out that way."

Clancy grunted again. "All right. Make sure all the doors and windows are secure now. We better contact Mr. Foster, let him know it looks like an attempted break-in."

"Will you catch him? And put him in jail?" Jeremy wanted to know. He did a little skip of excitement.

"Maybe," Clancy said. "You here alone with the kids, Darcy?"

"Yes, until the housekeeper comes home around four. She's having root canal work done."

Clancy was frowning. "We'll make sure everything's secure before we leave. You want to stay here, or should we take you all over to your own house?"

A part of me wanted to go home. What if a real burglar came back? He might not be scared by the alarm the next time, or he might feel he could steal whatever he was after before the police got there.

I didn't know how the Fosters would feel about my taking their kids somewhere else, though. And the kids weren't scared. Jeremy thought it was entertaining, and Melissa and Shana took their cue from him.

"I guess we'd better stay here, unless Mr. Foster thinks we should leave," I said slowly.

Clancy called the bank from the white telephone in the living room. Mr. Foster seemed satisfied that the police had routed the intruder, and Clancy assured him that they'd have a patrol car keeping an eye on the place for the rest of the day.

Clancy hung up the phone as the last of the officers returned to the house.

"Neighbors at the end of the block say a car

came out of the alley right after the alarm went off, but they didn't get a good look at it. All they're sure of is that it was dark, and probably five or six years old. Lady said she can't tell one model from another, but she thinks it was black."

Black. I remembered the car I'd thought followed Tim and me away from this house, and (maybe) the same one that had parked so the occupants could watch Irene and me when we went to the store. Could it have been the same one?

I opened my mouth to tell Clancy about the mysterious car, but he was already turning away, and Shana said firmly, "I have to go potty."

By the time Shana was taken care of, the police had gone. I stood looking at the phone, wondering if I should call Clancy and tell him about the car.

I'd feel stupid if it turned out to be just somebody who liked to look at girls. I knew Tim and his friends often drove around and watched girls.

But what if it wasn't only girl watchers?

I decided to call Tim. He'd know what to do.

I dialed our number, and Jimmy answered it. He didn't know where Tim was, he'd driven off ten minutes earlier. I swallowed and read off the Fosters' number for him to write down. "Tell Tim to call me when he comes back," I said, and Jimmy promised he would.

I felt a little better, which was a mistake. I didn't know Tim wasn't going to call back until it was too late.

Chapter Seven

Jeremy was so excited over the burglar alarm and the police coming that there was no way of calming him down. At least not any way that I could think of.

He whooped and hollered and raced around being a burglar, poking at his little sisters, instructing Melissa to be the intruder while he was the officer who pursued her. She got into the spirit of the thing, being about half really afraid, screaming as she ran to get away from him.

Shana didn't understand what was going on, but she ran and shrieked, too. After Melissa knocked over a lamp, I told them they'd better go out in the backyard. Luckily the lamp landed on the couch and it didn't break, but it looked expensive, and I didn't want to lose all my wages for the entire baby-sitting job over one lamp.

Jeremy was just as wild outside, but there was less to damage. I let him run and yell, as long as he didn't get too rough with his sisters.

After half an hour or so, though, I was getting tired of burglar alarm imitations and screaming, and Melissa fell and hurt her knee.

"Okay, that's enough," I said. "Come on, Melissa, we'd better wash that off and put disinfectant on it, and maybe a Band-aid."

Most little kids like Band-aids, and sure enough, she decided not to cry as I led her inside.

I found the medicine cabinet and was proud of the good job I did, getting the dirt off the scraped place, putting a Snoopy patch over it.

"Now maybe you can talk Jeremy into playing something quieter," I suggested.

There was an odd sound, then, and it took me a moment to identify it. The garage door opening? I'd heard it when Mrs. Murphy left; she had one of those devices you carry to open and close the garage doors without getting out of your car.

Was she back already? I was torn between relief that someone else could take on the job of calming Jeremy down and regret that my pay would be smaller if I went home early. The housekeeper was only scheduled for three more appointments after today, so I wasn't going to earn a whole lot anyway, I decided.

Just at that moment I heard a bellow of rage—or what sounded like rage—from somewhere else in the house. I sighed. Jeremy would have to be distracted by something else, I thought, and wondered what would work best. He had every game I'd ever heard of in his room, but he never seemed much interested in playing any of them except video games. I didn't dare play them with him because I had to watch the girls, too. Maybe I could think up something that just used his imagination, like the games my little brothers played all the time.

Melissa trotted off ahead of me with an exaggerated limp to make sure everyone knew she'd been injured. I lingered to wipe up the dirty fingermarks she'd made on the edge of the sink, then dropped the washcloth into the hamper.

I wondered how Diana was doing, up there in the tree house with only that old tattered book about child abuse to occupy her time. Maybe when I got home I'd go and talk to her, try to persuade her to confide in my folks. Kids can't do much about that kind of situation, but surely adults could. I didn't know if it was even legal for her to go and live with her brother or her aunt, but there must be some way to keep her from going back home where she was mistreated. My mom is usually pretty good about finding solutions to problems, even serious ones, and if Diana would talk to her . . .

I had walked back to the front hall, where I could see down the bedroom corridor and into the big living room. The house was so quiet now that I stopped, listening. Mom always said that the time she got most concerned was when she couldn't hear the kids making any noise, and I hoped the Fosters weren't into anything horrible or destructive.

Had Mrs. Murphy returned, or not? I didn't think I'd have noticed the neighbors operating a garage door opener, but maybe I'd mistaken the source of the sounds I'd heard. A new and alarming idea formed. What if it had been Jeremy doing something, not Mrs. Murphy at all?

Was there a control where he could get at it? I had a horrible vision of him opening the garage door and then closing it on Shana, though if anything like that happened, I'd surely have heard genuine screams instead of playful shrieks. Right now I wasn't hearing anything at all, and it made me uneasy.

"Jeremy? Melissa?" I called.

There was no response. Were they hiding, holding their hands over their mouths to restrain the giggles, waiting for me to walk by so they could jump out and pounce on me?

If I screamed when they did it, it could start another noisy game. If I didn't, they'd be disappointed. I walked back toward the kitchen, expecting to be startled any minute, trying to decide how to react.

Nothing sounded in the house except the grandfather clock in the corner of the dining room, which played a twelve-note tune and then chimed the hour. Three o'clock. At least an hour earlier than the housekeeper usually came home. I must have been mistaken about the noises.

I walked into the kitchen and stood in the middle of it, listening again. I could see through sliding glass doors out into the backyard, and there was no sign of the kids there.

And then I heard Shana's cry of distress, and perhaps anger. "I told you, I hafta go *potty*!"

Maybe that was it. Sometimes the older kids did look out for Shana, and they were probably all in the back bathroom. I started in that direction, about to call out again just as Shana cried, "I don't like you!"

Nobody'd given me permission to touch any of these kids for disciplinary purposes. Surely, though, if the older ones were tormenting Shana I'd be allowed to separate them, forcibly if I had to.

After the bright sunshine of the kitchen, the hallway seemed dim and shadowy. Shana was crying now, sobbing, and I quickened my steps. If they were hurting her, I was going to be tempted to—

I didn't see anybody in the short hallway

that ran off to the side of the main one, leading to Melissa's room. That door was closed, and it was almost dark in there; I didn't even glance that way in the urgency of reaching Shana and stopping whatever was being done to her. I'd forgotten I expected the kids to jump out and scare me.

When the hand closed over my mouth, from someone standing behind me, I made a smothered protest and tried to say, "Jeremy, cut it out!"

And then I realized it couldn't be Jeremy. The hand was too large, too strong, and there was an odor of tobacco that certainly didn't come from a six-year-old boy. And whoever held me against him was tall, a lot taller than I was.

Fear exploded in me. I tried to yelp and I struggled, until a harsh male voice said, "Knock it off, unless you want to get hurt!"

The burglar, I thought, he had gotten inside after all, and somehow the police didn't find him!

"Hurry up, what's going on?" another man's voice demanded, and I was trying to cope with the idea that there were two strange men here who had broken in when I heard the third voice.

"She had to go to the bathroom, so I thought I'd better take her. I didn't want to drag a kid around in wet pants," it said, and then the speaker appeared in front of me, in the bathroom door.

He was tall and skinny, with frizzled reddish brown hair and light blue eyes, and he was carrying Shana, whose small face was streaked with tears.

The second speaker appeared from behind me, so that my captor swiveled to face him. Number two was tall and thin, like the man carrying Shana, wearing worn jeans and a blue work shirt; they looked enough alike so I guessed they might be father and son, for this one was older than my dad. He scowled at me. "Who's this?"

"Baby-sitter," said my captor. "You didn't think the old lady went off and left the kids alone, did you? I told you, we watched this one before. We didn't want to come breaking in without knowing who was here. She's just a kid."

Inside my head all kinds of alarms were going off. I hadn't figured it out yet, but I knew it was bad. It wasn't a game, it was real, and it was scary.

I jerked hard to one side, and the hand slid off my mouth. "Who are you? What're you doing?" I demanded.

Shana pushed against the chest of the man who held her. "Put me down!" she demanded.

The man ignored her. "Come on, let's get out of here," he said. "This place makes me nervous. The cops were here before, they could come back."

The older man gave him a quelling look. "If you two hadn't been so stupid, they'd never have come in the first place."

The man behind me, the one I hadn't yet seen and who still had my arms pinned so I couldn't get away, put in his own comment. "We were smart enough to figure out a way in here, and it worked better than *your* way, Pa. What are we going to do with this one?"

My mind was racing. I knew I ought to be memorizing descriptions of them; instead I was so scared I could hardly think straight.

I tried to make myself calm down, but it was impossible. The man carrying Shana came on out into the hallway, and there was something about him that was sort of familiar. Frizzy reddish brown hair and pale blue eyes . . .

All of a sudden I knew who he was, who they all were, and I blurted it out as thoughtlessly as Jeremy would have done.

"You're Diana's brother!" I said, and then went cold as the silence, unbroken except for Shana's whimpering, grew around me.

The older man swore. "All right, you smart alecks," he said, sounding so angry I cringed away from him. "Now see what you went and done. Now we gotta get rid of the baby-sitter!"

For a minute I thought I was going to faint. On TV, when they say things like that, they mean they're going to drop someone in the lake, tied to a stone, or something else just as bad. We don't have any lake near us, but there's a river that I supposed would be just as fatal.

The one carrying Shana—I'd finally remembered his name, he was Dan—took on an expression that made me think I was right: they intended to dispose of me permanently.

"Hey, I agreed to the rest of this, but I'm not going to be up on any murder charge—"

"Don't be a sap," the brother behind me said. "Kidnapping's a federal offense, and you can't get any worse than that. But we don't need to do anything drastic. We'll just take her along. Might be handy, to look after the kids, save us the trouble."

"And what're we going to do later?" Diana's father demanded. "She's not only seen us, she knows who we are." I remembered what Mr. Hazen did to Diana, the bruises he'd left on her, and I felt cold all over. If he'd hurt his own kid, he wouldn't hesitate to hurt *us*.

"We're gonna leave this part of the country anyway, aren't we? As soon as they pay the ransom? We'll leave her tied up or something so she can't notify the police until we've had time to get out of the state. Once we've got money, we shouldn't have to worry about keeping away from them. Come on, let's get out of here."

He shoved me forward, and when I tried to

twist free (which only hurt, and didn't do any good) I got a look at him. Yes, it was Henry Hazen, Diana's older brother; he and Dan looked a lot alike, except that Henry didn't have as many freckles and he was probably five years older.

Why had I blurted out my recognition? If they hadn't known I'd recognized them, they'd have left me here. Tied up, maybe, but unharmed. Mrs. Murphy would have found me when she came home, and then I could have given the police their descriptions so they could go rescue the kids and arrest Mr. Hazen and his sons.

I was being propelled along the corridor toward the kitchen, then across the sunny room and into the garage. Behind me, I heard Dan say, "You bite me again, kid, and I'm going to smack you."

Mr. Hazen opened the door into the garage, and for a minute I thought that rescue was at hand, or at least that a decent adult had entered the picture. For there was Mrs. Murphy's car, the brown sedan she had driven off to the dentist's for her root canal work.

And then it dawned on me that the house-keeper was not there, for the doors of the car were opened, and there were Jeremy and Melissa inside. They each had a wide strip of tape over their mouths, and their eyes were wide with fear. Their hands had been tied together and secured to the door handles, so they couldn't escape.

Dan thrust Shana in beside them and climbed in back with the kids, slamming the door. "Let's go!" he said.

I was shoved into the front seat so roughly that I cracked my head; for a moment or two the pain of it blotted out everything else. And then I was aware that Henry had slid under the wheel, his father was pressed against me on the other side, and Henry was activating the garage door behind us with the control device.

We backed out onto the driveway, turning in the street, and headed toward the edge of town.

As the pain in my head receded, I knew the horrible truth: we were being kidnapped.

Chapter Eight

They hadn't put tape over my mouth, or Shana's, and from the back seat I heard her saying, "I want to go home."

I twisted around and saw her little face, lower lip stubbornly sticking out, as she glared at the man who held her. I saw, too, Jeremy and Melissa, whose eyes were oozing tears of fright, and I wanted to hug them, all three, and tell them it would be all right.

The trouble was, I didn't know if it would be all right or not. I wasn't crying, but it wasn't because I didn't feel like it.

Why hadn't I called to Clancy to wait, when he was leaving? When I couldn't get Tim at home, why hadn't I called the police then?

I tried to pull away from the men on either side of me, but there was nowhere to go.

Behind me, Dan told Shana, "Now, don't do that. It hurts, little girl, and I can't let you keep kicking me."

"My name's Shana," she informed him, and judging by the sounds she kicked him again, because he said, "All right, I'll have to hold your legs down, then."

Diana's father spoke suddenly in my ear. "You going to keep your mouth shut when we change cars, or do we have to tape your mouth, too?"

My mouth was so dry I could hardly speak. "What are you going to do with us?"

"Just keep you until Mr. Foster pays the ransom." It was Henry, who was driving, who answered. "No reason for you kids to get hurt; you just can't cause any trouble, understand?"

"You going to keep quiet?" Mr. Hazen asked, and I nodded. I didn't really think a promise made to a kidnapper was binding, anyway. If I got the chance to run or scream for help, I wouldn't hesitate for a second.

It didn't matter what I'd promised, or intended to do. When Mrs. Murphy's brown sedan turned into a narrow lane and stopped beside the black car we'd seen earlier, there was no one around to call to for help. There were only some poplar trees whispering in the breeze.

Far away, across a field, I saw a barn roof, but there were no people in sight. Screaming wouldn't gain me anything.

I'd been afraid of looking foolish if the driver of that black car had turned out to be innocent, so I'd kept still, and now look at me. Kidnapped, along with three little kids who suddenly didn't seem monstrous at all.

How long would it be before anyone discovered we were gone? Mrs. Murphy would probably come home in another hour or so—except that this was her car we were in, it was her door opener that had allowed these men into her garage.

Did that mean that Mrs. Murphy's car had been stolen while she was at the dentist, or was she somehow part of the plot? Could she have conspired with these three men to kidnap the Foster kids for ransom? Was one of them the man who'd come to the door, pretending to be a gas man? He'd been tall, too, and thin.

* * *

My head was aching and the blood pounded in my ears and made my heart feel as if it might beat its way out of my chest, too. No, I couldn't imagine the housekeeper plotting with these men. They'd been hanging around, had been watching the Foster house the day I'd come for an interview about the baby-sitting job, and then watching me, too. No doubt they'd figured out that Mrs. Murphy was going regularly for dental appointments, and that I'd be the only one in the house with three small kids. They'd failed to get in by passing as a gas man. Then they'd tried to break in earlier and been scared off by the burglar alarm; so they thought of stealing the housekeeper's car with the garage door opener in it.

They got out and dragged us with them. I looked at Jeremy and Melissa and couldn't help asking, "Couldn't you take the tape off their mouths?"

There was a moment's hesitation, and then Henry reached over and ripped off the tape, on first Jeremy and then Melissa. It pulled, and they both put up their hands to the places where the tape had stuck.

"I want to go home," Melissa said in a quavery voice, and moved closer to me. They'd loosened her wrists when she was taken out of the car, and she slid a small hand into mine, which I squeezed as reassuringly as I could.

"Come on," Pa Hazen said. "Get in the other car. Dan, you get rid of this one. We'll see you at the house."

This time I was shoved into the back seat of the black car with the Foster kids, and Henry again took the wheel, with his father sitting so he could watch us over the back of his seat.

"Don't try anything," he said, looking straight at me, and I swallowed hard. What was there to try that could possibly save us?

We were outside of town, in an area I'd ridden through but didn't know very well. There were farms and scattered farmhouses; we saw a man on a blue tractor and a few grazing sheep and cattle, but nobody who could rescue us.

The kids pressed close beside me, with Shana crawling into my lap. I didn't have enough hands to hug them all, so I sort of took turns. Their small bodies were warm and helpless against mine, and guilt washed over me. If

I'd used my head, talked to Clancy or Tim, or even the dispatcher at the police station, this wouldn't have happened.

It wasn't likely that the neighbors would have noticed anything amiss. If the Hazens had driven up in the black car, after the burglar alarm had gone off and the police had showed up, the people next door and across the street might have noticed. But who would pay any attention to Mrs. Murphy's familiar car, turning in the driveway and entering the garage?

When they realized we were missing, would anyone think to talk to Irene? She'd probably remember the license number of the black car. Only they'd know I'd disappeared from the Foster house, so they might not think of Irene at all. If the news came on at six and said we'd been kidnapped, her father would probably see it and tell her, and then they would call the police.

Only, I wasn't sure the reporters would have it yet. On a TV show I saw about a kidnapping, they didn't announce it on the news until after the ransom had been paid and the kidnapped child was freed. The kidnappers had told the parents not to call the police at all if they wanted to see their son alive again, though the people *had* secretly called the police.

I wondered if the Hazens had watched the same TV show. Marysville only gets two stations, so there isn't much choice of what to watch. I tried to think what I could do to escape. The victim on that TV show hadn't escaped. He'd had to be rescued by the police and the FBI, but the kidnapper had left some clues.

I didn't know if these kidnappers had left any clues or not.

Melissa leaned her head against my arm and whispered. "Are they going to shoot us, Darcy?"

"No, I don't think so," I said. "Don't be afraid. We're all together."

It was a stupid thing to say. We *were* all together, but there was nothing I could do to help any of us, and there seemed plenty of reason to be afraid. I didn't want the kids to cry or make a big fuss, though, for fear it would make the Hazens angry enough to hurt us.

My words seemed to make Melissa feel a

little better, though her dark eyes were still very large and she pressed herself tightly against me.

I glanced at Jeremy, on the other side. He watched TV, too, and I thought he probably had a better idea of the danger we were in than his sisters did; but now that his mouth wasn't taped, he didn't seem quite so scared. He was staring at the men in the front seat as if memorizing their descriptions, and I hoped he wouldn't blurt out the fact that he had done this, the way I had. Now that I'd had time to think, I was mortified that I'd been so stupid.

I tried to pay attention to where we were going, without being too obvious about it. It was hard to think with Pa Hazen watching me that way, but I did notice when we turned off the main road and headed toward a stand of woods. I thought I could find my way back out to that white farmhouse where there would be a phone. All I had to do was escape.

When I saw where we were going, my heart sank. Escaping wasn't going to be easy.

We had driven a short distance through the woods when we came to a stone wall with a wrought iron gate in it. Pa Hazen got out and unlocked the gate and opened it so Henry could drive the car through. When we were through, Pa Hazen closed the gate behind us and got back in the car, but he didn't relock the gate. So Dan could get in, I guessed, but my heart was beating faster.

If I had a chance to run, should I go for help by myself? Or would I put the children in worse danger by leaving them behind? Shana was so little she couldn't possibly run very far and heavy enough so she'd really slow me down if I tried to carry her. I wished my head didn't still ache from bumping it; maybe then I could think better.

Inside the walls the trees were farther apart, and there was overgrown grass between them. As we drove toward the house, I was impressed by its size and graceful lines, but when Dan stopped the car before the front door, I could see that the pale red bricks were crumbling and the paint was peeling on the windowframes. It didn't look as if anyone lived there anymore.

"All right, get out," Pa Hazen said, and we

sort of stumbled out into the sunshine and were herded up the shallow steps and into the house.

For a minute I felt blind in the shadowy hallway, and then things came into focus. There was a big entry hall with stairs rising from one side of it and huge sliding doors leading to rooms on each side. I didn't see much in the way of furniture, except an old sofa in one room that looked as if the mice had been at it; the stuffing was falling out of it.

"Upstairs," Pa Hazen said, and I moved quickly so he wouldn't touch me again. Henry carried Shana, who, though she stuck out her lower lip, didn't argue with him, and I held onto Melissa and Jeremy; the stairs were plenty wide enough so we could walk three abreast.

"In there," Henry said, and we went where he directed, into a large room with nothing in it except an old mattress on the floor.

He put Shana down, and I envied the cool look she gave him. "I don't like you," she told Henry, and he stared at her.

"I don't like you much, either," he returned,

"but it doesn't matter. We don't have to like each other. You just stay put here; and if your daddy pays us the money we're gonna ask for, then you can go home. Just don't try anything." This last part was said to me, and then Henry went out and locked the door behind him.

I stared around the room. There were big windows on two sides, but they didn't offer any hope. We must have been thirty feet off the ground, and though there was a roof beneath one of the windows, it was very steep and too high for us to drop from without breaking our necks. There were no sheets or blankets to tear into strips to make a rope to slide down, no tree branches close enough to the house to provide an escape.

Nothing at all.

For a moment my throat ached so much I thought I would cry. Only I knew I couldn't do that; it would scare the kids. I'd have to pretend I thought everything was going to be fine.

"What are we going to do?" Jeremy asked.

I looked at the mattress. "Well, all we have is a gym mat. I guess we're going to do calisthenics."

"What's 'thenics?" Melissa wanted to know.

"Gym exercises," Jeremy said. "Isn't it?"

I got them going on some of the Yoga exercises my mom does to keep her figure, and then some jumping jacks. We stirred up enough dust to make me sneeze, but the kids weren't looking scared anymore.

I wished I had a watch so I'd know how much time had passed. Had Mrs. Murphy reported her car stolen yet? Had anyone found it, or had Dan hidden it too well? Was my mom wondering why I hadn't come home for supper? Had anyone notified the police that the Foster kids and I were missing?

"I have to go potty," Shana said.

I looked around the room. There was no provision for this, and they hadn't brought any spare clothes for the kids. There was no telling how long we'd be here. On TV the kidnappers usually make the parents sweat it out for a while before they even make their ransom demands, and the parents have to have time to get the money. Could a bank president like Mr. Foster get the money quicker than ordinary people? And then they have to drive out in the dark to some isolated place to leave a bag containing the cash. After the kidnappers have the money, they are supposed to leave the kids where someone will find them soon, after they've made their getaway.

I didn't know if these kidnappers would follow the TV scripts, but I had to assume we'd be here for a day or two, at least. I tried not to let my heart sink any lower than it already was.

If we were going to be cooped up here, we'd all need to use the bathroom.

I walked to the door and pounded on it, making such a racket it almost scared me all over again. "Hey! We need to use the bathroom!"

I wouldn't have been surprised if they'd ignored me, but they didn't. I heard footsteps on the stairs, and then Dan opened the door.

"It's across the hall," he said, pointing, and stood waiting while we went over there.

The bathroom was about the size of my bedroom at home. There was a big, old-fashioned tub on legs and faded linoleum and rust stains on everything; the water ran in a trickle when you turned it on. Jeremy said he didn't need to go, but I told him he'd better, because there was no telling when they'd let us come here again.

When we went back into the hallway, I worked up my courage and spoke to Dan. "If you're going to keep us here very long, we've got to be able to go back and forth to the bathroom. Even during the night," I added, not knowing if it was true or not. "Shana will need to go."

Dan looked uncertain. "We can't let you run loose."

"You can't leave us locked up without a bathroom," I said, hoping I sounded firm enough to be convincing.

"I'll have to talk to Pa and Henry," he decided. "For now, I gotta lock you in again."

About ten minutes later I heard footsteps on the stairs again, so my hopes were raised.

Dan opened the door and let it stand wide. "Okay, you can go back and forth to the bathroom, but don't try to go downstairs. If you do, they'll tear your legs off."

I walked to the doorway and looked out. There at the top of the stairs lay two gigantic Doberman pinschers.

"Guard," Dan told them, and turned and went back down the stairs.

I stared at the dogs. They blocked the top of the stairway and looked at me with yellowish eyes, saliva dripping from their mouths, which showed long, sharp fangs.

Jeremy came up beside me and looked out, too, and the Dobermans stared back and growled, deep in their throats.

I made myself speak and wondered if I was successful in sounding off hand. "Well, I guess we won't be going downstairs."

The dogs didn't move, but they lay looking at us with the meanest eyes I ever saw.

Chapter Nine

It didn't take very long for the kids to get bored in the room with the mattress. They'd been scared, but since nothing terrible had happened to us—except being carried away by these strangers to an old deserted house in the country—they gradually got over the worst of their fright.

The same wasn't true of me. It was impossible not to remember that I'd told the men I knew who they were. How could they dare to let me go, even after they'd collected a ransom? Even if I promised never to tell—and I'd have promised anything at this stage—they couldn't be sure I'd keep the promise. They might turn the kids free eventually, but what would they have to do with me?

Irene used to sit behind me in study hall

and concentrate on making me turn around, and quite often I'd done it. I wondered if I could make *her* think of *me* and remember that license number and tell it to the police. I tried concentrating on sending her that message, until Jeremy poked me in the shoulder.

"There's nothing to do," he said.

I resisted telling him how lucky he was that we didn't have something awful to do, as might have been the case. I didn't really want him scared again, which meant I'd have to pretend I wasn't afraid, either.

"I'm sorry. Sit down, and I'll tell you a story," I offered.

I recited a story I'd once read to the Martino girls; Jeremy and Melissa paid attention, but Shana didn't. The next thing I knew she was standing in the doorway looking out.

"Big doggies," she observed.

"Stay away from them," I told her quickly. "They're guard dogs, and they won't let us down the stairs." I didn't want to upset her by suggesting they'd bite her.

She seemed entranced with them, even when, as she stepped across the threshold into the hallway, they lifted their heads and growled again, deep in their powerful throats.

"Shana, come back," I said, and was relieved when she edged into the bedroom again. She still didn't look scared, though. Just thoughtful.

The older kids didn't want another story. "I want to play something," Jeremy said.

"Okay. Let's play hide the thimble. We don't have a thimble, so we'll have to use something else." I looked around for an object that would work. "Melissa, could we use one of your barrettes?"

She wore little red plastic ones that went with her red plaid dress. She took one out of her hair and gave it to me.

"All right. Both of you turn your backs—you, too, Shana—and I'll hide it, and then you can all look for it," I told them.

Jeremy found it, hidden at the foot of the mattress, and then Melissa found it on the windowsill. Jeremy didn't want to play any more.

"There aren't enough places to hide it," he said, which was true, so we put it into Melissa's hair again.

"Where's Shana?" Jeremy asked, and I spun around, looking. The little girl was out in the middle of the hallway this time, only a couple of yards from the Dobermans.

"Shana, come here!" I called, and then I realized the dogs weren't growling at her; they were simply alert, watching.

"Maybe we could explore the upstairs," Jeremy suggested. "See, they're letting Shana go along the hall."

I was leery at first, because I certainly didn't want to tangle with those dogs, but when we all moved outside the door, heading toward the bathroom, the animals did nothing except watch us. Maybe we *could* get away with exploring.

The kids just wanted something to do. *I* wanted a way out of the house, if I could find one.

So we checked out the bathroom, where the dogs were content to let us go. There was one window, painted shut, that opened on another section of roof. Carefully, watching the dogs, I took a step along one of the side halls.

They let us go. We explored the whole second

floor. One door opened onto a steep, narrow stairway that must lead to an attic, but it was so dark in there I didn't want to try that. There were six big, dusty rooms on our floor, none of them with anything in them except a few odds and ends of junk. I couldn't see how a broken chair or a dresser with the veneer peeling off or a box of old *National Geographics* from 1942 could help us escape.

The magazines did have interesting pictures, though. We hauled the box back to the room with our mattress in it, and for a little while we stayed busy looking at pictures of naked children in Africa and gaily costumed dancers in Czechoslovakia and some brightly colored birds with big beaks that inhabited the jungles of South America.

And then we came to a story on a Hawaiian luau, with full-color pictures of a roast pig and all kinds of fruit and vegetables. Jeremy looked at it and said, "I wonder if they're going to feed us."

I was wondering, myself. It wasn't dark out yet, but I knew by my stomach that it was way past mealtime.

113

It wasn't long after that that Dan brought us our supper. It came in two paper bags that made the dogs lift their heads and sniff as he stepped between them.

The kids looked at him when he handed me one sack. "Do you have any little kids?" Shana wanted to know.

Dan shook his head. "Nope. I'm not married. I didn't know if the kids would like onions, so I had them leave them off."

The bag gave off a savory aroma when I opened it and handed out hamburgers. They were still warm, so I thought he must have bought them fairly close by. The kids sat on the edge of the mattress as I handed them out, breaking one in half for Shana after I'd tucked a paper napkin at the neck of her dress so the juice wouldn't drip down her front.

She accepted that, and the little packet of french fries, then looked up at Dan Hazen. "Where's the ketchup?"

"It's in there, in little paper tubs," he told her. He even reached in, got one and opened it for her, and Shana began to eat contentedly, dipping each piece of potato into the sauce.

"I got pop, not milk," Dan said, and opened the other sack to hand out cold cans.

I wasn't too scared to be hungry, and I sat down beside the kids to eat my share. Dan stood there uncertainly. "You think you'll need a blanket or anything tonight?"

It was pretty warm, but my heart quickened. "It gets cool before morning," I said. If I had a blanket, maybe I could make a rope of it to hang out a window.

"I'll get one of Okie's," he said.

Jeremy spoke though a mouthful of hamburger.

"Who's Okie?"

"He's the old guy that's the caretaker of this place." Dan had apparently decided to stay for a few minutes; he squatted down near Shana and used a napkin to wipe off her chin.

"What's a caretaker?"

"Somebody who takes care of something. He's an old man who lives in a room at the back, downstairs, and keeps vandals from getting in."

"What's vandals?" Jeremy wanted to know. At least when he was asking questions, he wasn't bored or scared, I thought.

"Well, they're . . . uh, vandals break windows and steal things," Dan said.

"There's nothing to steal here," Jeremy pointed out.

"Yeah, I know, but the owner doesn't want the windows broken, things like that."

"Where is he now?" Melissa asked. She, too, was deliberately coating each french fry with ketchup before she ate it.

"Okie's in the hospital. Having an operation. He'll be gone a week or two," Dan said; and I knew why they'd felt safe in bringing us here. The house had no close neighbors, and it would be empty, except for us, long enough for the Hazens to collect the ransom. Probably, I thought, spirits sinking, nobody else would ever come here at all.

"How come you're in Okie's house?" Jeremy wanted to know. He didn't bother to stop eating when he spoke.

"It isn't his house; he just works here, making sure nobody bothers anything. He asked me to feed his dogs, so I got a key. Don't spill that—"

He stopped talking, because the can of pop

had already been knocked over and was making a dark puddle between Melissa's feet. She looked at it with dismay.

"My shoes are wet."

"Move over that way, and I'll get something to wipe it up," Dan said, and left to get a towel from the bathroom for the job.

"Are those Okie's dogs?" Jeremy wanted to know as soon as Dan came back.

"Yeah. They're trained guard dogs." Dan swiped away at the floor. "Don't mess with them. They bite."

He straightened up, holding the sodden towel. "I'll bring a blanket before it's time to go to sleep."

After he'd gone, we finished eating, except that Shana had left a lot of her hamburger. She stood up, and before I could move to stop her, she walked out into the hall and dropped the mangled remains of her food on the floor in front of the nearest dog.

For a moment the Doberman did nothing, though his nose quivered. A trained guard dog probably wouldn't touch anything that wasn't given to him by his master, I thought.

But then the dog shifted position, ever so slightly, and bent his head, snaking out a tongue to pull the hamburger and bun into his mouth. Saliva dripped from the other dog's mouth.

I hadn't finished my own supper, and I was still hungry, but I stopped eating. If we could bribe the dogs—

The minute I approached, the dogs growled, and I paused. "Good dogs," I said. I guess I wasn't very convincing, because they growled again.

"I do it," Shana said, and took the rest of my sandwich. Very carefully, she placed it on the floor in front of the second dog, and a moment later it was gone.

Would it be possible to win over the dogs with food? So far, it was only Shana they had allowed near them, though, and then only to drop something for them to eat. As long as any of us were in sight, the Dobermans kept their heads up, alert and ready to spring to their feet. I didn't think it was likely they'd let us past them, not even Shana, and what could a two-and-a-half year old do on her own?

The big house was so still. Except for the noises we made ourselves, I hadn't heard anything. Were all three men downstairs, or had some of them gone away? The more of them there were, the harder it would be to outwit them.

It was dusk, now; the shadows grew in the hall and in the corners of the room. A single naked bulb dangled from the middle of the ceiling, and I flicked the switch beside the door to make sure the electricity was on. The idea of sitting in the dark didn't appeal to me very much.

Shana came and crawled into my lap as I sat on the mattress. "Sing, Darcy," she said sleepily.

I don't have a good singing voice, and usually I only sing along with enough other people to make sure nobody can hear me. Singing for little kids didn't make me self-conscious, though; they weren't a critical audience.

I held her and sang a few songs, and Shana got heavier and heavier. When her head flopped over, I stretched her out on the mattress, and then went over and turned off the light.

"Are we all going to have to sleep on that one bed?" Jeremy asked.

"Unless you want to sleep on the floor," I told him. "We'll all fit if we're careful. Do you want to lie down and go to sleep now, too?"

It was almost dark in the room; I hadn't left the overhead light on, because it would be shining right in the face of anyone who lay down. I couldn't see the dogs at the top of the stairs, nor hear them, but I knew they were still there.

Melissa slid her small, warm hand into mine. "I want to go home," she said.

A lump came into my throat. "I'd like to go home, too. Only I don't think they're going to let us go right away. Would you like me to sing you to sleep, too?"

She was quite a bit bigger than Shana, but she sat close to my side and listened to me sing. Every time I'd stop, Jeremy would suggest another song, and some of them he sang with me. None of this woke Shana up.

"Somebody's coming," Jeremy said suddenly, just as Melissa was easing back beside her little sister.

One of the dogs whined, and I leaned forward to peer through the open doorway, hoping it wasn't Pa Hazen. I was more afraid of him that I was of Dan or even Henry.

It was Dan. He turned on a light on the landing, such a small dirty bulb that its glow didn't come very far into our room. He handed me a blanket. "Here. You might as well all go to sleep."

I felt like telling him that was easier said than done, but I didn't. Maybe if they thought I was still too terrified to think, or too stupid, they'd get careless, and there'd be a chance for me to escape.

Meekly, I said, "Thank you."

I jumped when Jeremy spoke in a loud voice. "We want to go home."

"Well, you can't, not for a few days," Dan told us. "We haven't even called your dad yet about the ransom. We're gonna do that about two o'clock in the morning, and then he'll have to have time to get the money and bring it. So you might as well go to sleep."

Two o'clock in the morning. Just like in that TV movie. Timed to have everybody's nerves on edge and keep them from sleeping the whole night, so they couldn't think very well. Surely the Fosters would have called in the police by now, but were there any clues for them to follow?

"We're not going to have to stay up here in this room all day tomorrow, are we?" Jeremy demanded. "There's nothing to do."

"I don't know. I don't think Pa wants you downstairs," Dan said. He turned and left the room, calling the dogs. "Come on, you want to run for a few minutes?"

The Dobermans sprang up, tails wagging, and followed him down the stairs.

I looked at the blanket and gave a tentative tug at the edge of it. Torn lengthwise into strips that could be tied together, would it make a rope long enough for me to slide down to the ground from that back roof?

It was too dark now to see if there was anything to tie an end to, and I couldn't tear it, anyway. In the movies people can tear a strip off anything—a blanket, a shirt, a petticoat—but this was too strong a fabric. Without scissors to get a tear started, I didn't think I could do it.

"The dogs are gone," Jeremy said softly, starting out into the pale light on the landing that showed the top of the stairs. "Maybe we could get out and run away."

I could hear the pulses pounding in my ears, just thinking about it. "I don't think we'd make it," I said. "He's got the dogs running loose outdoors, I think. They'd know if we got out of the house, and it's a long way to another house."

"Are we just going to sit here, then?" he wanted to know. "Aren't we going to try to escape?"

"Maybe later," I told him. "Let them get a false sense of security, thinking we're too scared to act. Jeremy, if I could get away, would you take care of your sisters, keep them from being scared, until I could get help and come back? I could go farther, faster, by myself, than trying to take all of you. Shana's so little, she'd really slow us down; but we couldn't leave her alone. She'd have to have you to take care of her."

His eyes were very large in the dim light. "I guess I could," he said finally. "Only I'd rather we all run away together."

"Me, too," I agreed. "We'll have to wait and see."

After a while, Jeremy stretched out beside Melissa and went to sleep.

I thought about home, and Clancy, and Irene, who might give him a clue if she knew I was missing, and hoped that when Mr. Foster handed over the ransom money the Hazens would really let us all go.

But I couldn't stop being afraid that they wouldn't.

Chapter Ten

I couldn't sleep. I sat on the edge of that old mattress, listening to the quiet breathing of the kids beside me, and I could see the place where the Dobermans had been at the top of the stairs, before Dan took them out for a run.

He hadn't brought them back yet. It was fully dark now, except for that one small bulb on the second floor landing. Irene, Irene, I thought, tell Clancy or somebody about the black car and its license number. Get us out of here.

Downstairs, a telephone rang.

I came bolt upright. It sounded very far away, as if it was behind closed doors, but I was sure it was a telephone. It rang three times before it stopped.

If I could get to a telephone and call the police, or my dad, or anybody—

They would take care that I didn't reach the phone, of course. Still . . .

I got up quietly and stepped into the hallway. The stairs went down into darkness, and after a moment's hesitation, I began to ease down the steps, clinging to the railing.

I expected the stairs would creak, but they didn't. They were very high compared to the ones at home, and it took me a long time to reach the bottom.

It wasn't as totally dark down there as I'd expected, for a faint light filtered through to the entry hall from a room far at the back of the house.

The front door was right there, and I was glad I was wearing running shoes with rubber soles that didn't make any noise as I moved toward it. If anybody had come up behind me as I reached for the knob, I wouldn't have heard them, my heart was pounding so hard.

The door was locked, of course. I'd known it would be, yet disappointment almost made me sick to my stomach. A window, then?

There were two windows, one on each side of the door, that opened onto the veranda. I tried each of them, but they'd been painted shut years ago. I might have broken the glass if I'd had anything heavy to hit it with, but the men in the back of the house would have heard that and caught up with me before I got down the porch steps. Even if they couldn't see me, those dogs would find me before I ran down to the gate, and probably that had been relocked by now, anyway.

No way out here, I thought. I could have gone back up to that almost-empty bedroom upstairs, but instead I began to move slowly and cautiously toward the source of light at the rear of the house.

I turned a corner and saw a slice of brightly lighted kitchen. It was old-fashioned looking, with worn linoleum on the floor and wooden chairs at a big table with a green and white plastic tablecloth over it.

When a door opened and closed, I froze against the wall, not daring to go either forward or backward. Henry's voice sounded so near that the hair stood up on the back of my neck.

"Did I hear the phone?"

"Yeah, it was Pa. He said there was nothing

on the evening news. I bet the Fosters called the cops, though." Dan sounded nervous.

"It doesn't matter if they did." Henry didn't sound nervous at all. "The housekeeper doesn't know what happened to her car. They probably haven't even found it yet, where you left it in the gravel pit. You wiped all the prints off the steering wheel and the door handles, didn't you?"

"Sure. I still think the gravel pit's too close to here, though. They might get wise that I walked away from it and wouldn't have gone too far."

"Why should they?" I heard another door closing and figured out that it was a cupboard door. Henry crossed the band of light and poured himself coffee from a pot on the stove. "They won't be able to tell you walked away instead of changed cars."

He took his cup to the table and sat down, where I could see a little bit of his back. It made me feel somewhat safer not to have him moving around, though Dan was out of sight and could have come through the doorway any minute. Where, I wondered, was the telephone?

"I don't know," Dan replied. "It's just so

close here, I feel like they might guess where we are, when they find the old lady's car."

"No reason they should come here," Henry told him. "Everybody in the neighborhood knows old Okie is the caretaker, and he lets the dogs run free on the grounds. Even the kids don't try anything since he got the dogs. The place is a mile and a half from the nearest neighbor, anyway, and nobody can tell if there's traffic in and out or more lights than usual. Okie didn't tell anybody but us that he was going to the hospital for a week or two, and nobody'd suspect *him* of kidnapping."

"He's going to be pretty mad when he finds out we used this house for a hideout," Dan observed. I heard the clatter of a cup against something and guessed he was drinking coffee, too.

"Why should he ever know? We'll be gone before he comes back. I doubt if he goes upstairs once a year, and even if he does, what will there be for him to see? An old mattress. He probably won't remember if it was there before or not."

Dan didn't seem any happier. "I just wish

this was all over. Even if we get the ransom money—"

"What do you mean, *if* we get it? Foster'll pay, all right, as soon as we tell him how much and where to deliver it," Hank interrupted.

"—we can't just go on about our business, here in Marysville, like we planned at first. Not since that babysitter knows who we are."

"Don't worry about the sitter," Hank told him, and it made me so cold I clamped my jaws to keep my teeth from chattering.

"Listen, I'm not going to hurt any kids," Dan said, and he sounded as if he'd said it before. "Holding 'em for ransom is one thing, but hurting 'em is something else. You know, if Ma ever finds out about this, she's going to kill us all."

Henry snorted. "Ma's scared of the old man; she wouldn't do anything even if she found out, which she's not going to do. Not unless you're stupid enough to tell her, and then it'll be *Pa* who'll kill you. This is rotten coffee; is it some Okie left, or did you make it?"

They talked about the coffee, and the food, and then about how long they had to wait until they could call Mr. Foster and ask for the money. Dan wanted to call sooner, but Henry said they had to wait until two a.m., the way Pa Hazen had instructed.

"Means we can't even go to bed until so late," Dan grumbled, and I wondered how they could sleep, under the circumstances.

His brother changed the subject, getting up to dump the last of his coffee into the sink. "You have any trouble with the kids while I was gone?"

"No. I brought the dogs inside, to guard the stairs, because they said they had to use the bathroom. They won't get past the dogs."

Henry swung around from the sink. "The dogs are outside. They came up to me when I drove in."

"Yeah, I know. They'd been guarding for hours; I had to let 'em run before I lock up for the night. It's a good thing they got a little bit used to us when we were here taking down those trees and sawing 'em up. They still make me nervous. Every time I turn my back, I expect one of 'em to nip my heels."

"So if the dogs are outdoors, who's watching the kids?" Henry demanded.

"They're asleep, and besides, they can't get out. Every outside door in the place is locked except the one you just came in, and that's been in my sight all the time. And the windows don't open, either, except that one in Okie's bedroom. They can't get at that without coming through the kitchen. So what're you worrying about?"

"Your stupidity, mostly," Henry said. "If anything happens to screw this up, we're all going to jail. You know that, don't you?"

"You and Pa promised that wouldn't happen."

"Not if you do things right. But you let that girl run away and bring back the police, and I guarantee they'll lock us up for a long time. You didn't want to hang around this town forever, doing odd jobs, without any money, any more than we did. Anybody said, 'Mexico, with plenty of cash,' and you got as excited as the rest of us. You better check on those kids, and I'll get the dogs back in here."

I started backing up, moving as quickly as I could without making any racket. I had to be up there in that room by the time Dan got there; if they found me downstairs, they might very well tie me up, and then all hope of escape would be gone.

I reached the stairs and fled upwards as fast as I could go. I had barely stretched out on the mattress beside Melissa when I heard Dan on the stairs. I squeezed my eyes shut and hoped my breathing wouldn't give away the fact that I'd raced up there just ahead of him.

Chapter Eleven

I could feel them standing there, looking at me.

I heard the dogs, too, their toenails clicking on the wooden floor. My heart thundered in my ears.

"You better be more careful from now on," Henry said. "Don't take any chances, you hear? All we have to do is keep the kids here until Foster hands over the money, and it'll all be over. So stay cool, Dan. Just watch these kids so they don't get away."

"They're not gonna get away," Dan said, and he sounded annoyed.

After a minute or so, they went away.

I opened my eyes. They'd left the hall light on, and the dogs were back on guard duty.

I wanted to go to sleep, but I couldn't. I lay there beside the Foster kids, and after a while it cooled off enough so I put the blanket over them.

It was partly my fault they were here, I thought. If nobody came to rescue us, how could I get them out of this? And myself with them?

I guess I did sleep for a while, only I kept waking up. Each time I knew at once where I was, and what was happening. I wondered if Henry had called Mr. Foster yet, and how long it would take to get the ransom money together and deliver it.

And what they'd do with me, when they were ready to take their money and run to Mexico.

Finally I woke up and there were birds twittering in the trees outside. The kids began to wake up then, too, and we all trooped to the bathroom. We couldn't brush our teeth or comb our hair, but we washed our faces. The dogs kept their heads up and watched us as we went back to the bedroom; they weren't growling the way they had done last night, though.

It was still pretty early, and we didn't hear any sounds from downstairs. Jeremy stood looking out the window. "Maybe I could crawl out on the roof and drop down and go for help," he suggested.

"It's not as easy as in the movies," I told him, trying not to sound as depressed as I felt. "It's an awful long way down, and you might break a leg or something. I thought of trying to make a rope out of the blanket, but I can't tear it. I don't see anything to tie it to, anyway." I stood beside him, wishing the house wasn't so high off the ground, wishing for a miracle.

Melissa said, "I want to go home."

I knew just how she felt. "They probably called your daddy last night. Maybe it won't be long before they let us go," I told her.

Shana said, "I'm hungry."

"I'm bored," Jeremy added. "Darcy, let's go exploring again."

"We already explored, yesterday, remember? All we found was some old magazines."

"We didn't explore upstairs. Maybe there's something up there. A gun that we could shoot them with."

That wasn't likely, but I didn't have any

better suggestion. "Okay," I said, "if the dogs will let us open the door to the attic stairs."

Though the Dobermans watched us warily, they didn't growl when we crept quietly along the hallway toward the door to the stairs. It wasn't very light in the stairway, but a faint illumination came from above, enough so we could climb without falling.

Jeremy went first, then Melissa, then Shana and me. We emerged into a great dusty room with all kinds of junk in it, mostly old trunks and broken furniture. Again, though, none of it looked like anything we could use. Even the windows were dirty, so dirty we couldn't see much through them.

I was trying to open a window so I could see more clearly when Jeremy found some kind of old fur lap robe and draped it over his head and down his back. "I'm a monster, and I'm going to eat you for my breakfast!" he cried, and dove toward his sisters.

Both of them shrieked as if he really were a great animal about to devour them. Shana grabbed my leg, and I put an arm around her, but Melissa ran, crashing into a bird cage and several boxes that teetered and fell, spilling old clothes and papers over the attic floor.

"Jeremy, cut it out! We don't want to make enough racket so they'll hear us on the ground floor," I told him, and to my relief he stopped chasing Melissa.

She didn't realize he'd come to a halt, though, and she careened into an old mattress that stood on end against one wall. It toppled with a cloud of dust that made us all sneeze.

"Boy, I'm glad they didn't bring this one down for us to sleep on," I said, and shoved it off Melissa, who had been knocked down by it. "It's all right, don't *yell*, Melissa!"

"Hey, look!" Jeremy said, letting the furry thing slide off his shoulders. "There's a funny little door!"

There was. It was small enough that I would have to duck to go through it. "It's probably just a storage area." I said, and would have turned around to go back downstairs.

Jeremy, however, wanted to know what was behind it. He tugged at it, then turned to me. "Help me, Darcy. Let's see what's inside. Maybe they hid a treasure in there!"

"There'll only be more junk," I predicted, only it wasn't trash that was revealed when I jerked open the door, but another set of stairs.

They were so steep and narrow they were almost a ladder, and they curled around like the stairs I'd once seen inside a lighthouse we visited on Lake Huron.

"Let's see what's up there," Jeremy suggested, sounding excited, and I wished I could forget that we were prisoners in this big old house and just enjoy myself.

Well, having the kids interested in exploring seemed better than having them crying in terror. I followed them up the stairs, helping Shana because she couldn't make it on her own.

Above me, I heard Jeremy's delighted cry. "It's a little room! Boy, I wish we had one like this in our house!"

A cupola, I realized, gaining the top of the stairs, a round room at the top of the house. It had been used as a children's playroom, for there were still toys there.

"A shicken," Shana announced, and headed for the other side of the room. There was a table and four chairs, small-child size, and a miniature stove and sink and ice box. They weren't modern like the ones the kids had at home, but they were toys, coated with dust. At the table sat a doll with its hair mostly worn away, a teddy bear with one eye, and a clown doll made out of a sock that sagged limply over a tiny china plate.

"We can play house, Melissa said, lifting a teapot and pretending to pour into a blue and white cup.

"There's a train," Jeremy said, and dropped to his knees on the dusty floor. "Only there's no place to plug it in!"

"It's not electric," I told him, and moved toward one of the windows that opened on all sides.

He gave me a puzzled look. "How does it work, then?"

"I guess you just have to push it around the track by hand," I told him, but I wasn't thinking about the train. I was thinking how isolated this place was.

It felt as if we were a mile above the ground. We could see way off over the unmowed lawns, through the trees, to the stone wall that surrounded the place; there were no houses within sight beyond the wall, only more trees, though there was one thing that might be worth investigating if I could get outside the house.

It probably wouldn't even show from the ground, but from above we could make out a break in the stone wall, with a gate set into it. I wondered if that gate, too, was locked. Or if, because it was hidden in shrubbery on both sides of the wall, it might be possible to open it and escape that way.

For some reason the windows up there weren't painted shut, the way they were in the rest of the house, though I had to shove hard to get one open. We needed the fresh air, because it was hot up at the top of the house. The roofs spread out all around us, and we could have walked on these for they were almost flat; only there was nowhere to go.

I opened a couple more windows. I didn't think it was a good idea to stay up here for long, because I didn't know how the Hazens would feel about it and I didn't want to antagonize them, not while there was a chance I might be able to outwit them if they weren't expecting me to do it. Yet the kids were being entertained for a little while, and I hated to chase them out of the special room immediately. I'd have liked it myself if I hadn't been a prisoner.

Jeremy was entertaining himself in a way that nearly gave me a heart attack when I saw him.

I turned around from looking out over the grounds and saw him at one of the open windows, a toy arrow in one hand, stretching out to poke at something up under the eaves.

At first all I thought about was that he'd fall out and roll over the edge of the roof below. But then I saw what he was trying to poke with the arrow.

"Jeremy! Stop it!" I cried, and made a grab for him.

He turned to me with a smile of pure, innocent delight. "It's a bee's nest, Darcy. Isn't it?"

"Wasps, I think. Get away from there. They sting, and it hurts something awful. I remember, because my brother knocked a nest off the corner of our garage once, and we all got stung."

His smile faded, "I never saw a bee's nest.

I just wanted to poke a little hole in it and see what happened."

I took the arrow out of his hand and dropped it near the bow, which couldn't have been used to shoot because it was broken. "What happens when you poke a hole in the nest is that the wasps all come swarming out and sting everybody in sight. Come on, we'd better get back before they discover we're missing. We don't want to make them mad so they get nasty."

The only thing I let them take downstairs was a box of old children's books. I carried them back down to the second floor, and we started looking through them, to take our minds off being hungry.

"I want *Greg'ry Gray and the Brave Beast*," Shana said, and we tried to explain to her that that book wasn't among the ones we had. Instead, we read about a goat named Billy Whiskers and some kittens named Buzz, Fuzz, Suzz, and Agamemnon.

Shana picked up some of the words and sang them softly under her breath. "Happy birthday, mew mew." She giggled to herself.

After a while Dan came upstairs, carrying

more paper bags. "Breakfast," he announced.

I was hungry enough to eat just about anything, but Shana stuck out her lower lip at the sight of the hamburgers. "No," she said when I offered her one. "Go shicken."

Dan stared at her, exasperated. "I'll get chicken next time. For now, this is all we got."

"Go *shicken*!" Shana insisted, looking as if she were going to cry.

"I think she means *kitchen*," Jeremy translated. "She likes cereal for breakfast."

"Fruit Loops," Shana stated. "I want Fruit Loops."

"Me, too," Melissa agreed. She often took her cue from one of the other kids.

"Why can't we go downstairs and eat?" Jeremy wanted to know. "Maybe there's some cereal down there."

Dan hesitated. "I'm supposed to keep you up here."

"Why?" I asked. "You're going to have to let the dogs outdoors for a few minutes, aren't you? So they can't guard us all the time. Shana will be a lot easier to handle if she gets what she wants to eat."

144

I was sure his brother would never have let us talk him into it, but Dan finally shrugged. "Okay, Come downstairs to eat. But don't try anything."

I couldn't think of anything to try that had any chance of working, but I kept watching for an opportunity. We sat around the kitchen table, where Jeremy and I ate hamburgers, and the girls had cereal. There weren't any Fruit Loops, only bite-size shredded wheat, the kind my dad calls "grown-up cereal." While we were eating, I located the telephone on the wall beside the stove. I just glanced at it, then quickly away, so Dan wouldn't think I was plotting anything.

"When can we go home?" Jeremy asked.

"When your daddy gives us the money tonight," Dan said. There were dirty dishes in the sink, so he must have already had something to eat. I wondered if they were going to leave them there for the old man called Okie, when he came home from the hospital.

"Did you talk to Daddy?" Jeremy demanded.

"Henry did. He'll get the money this morning. After dark he'll meet us and hand it over, and then you can go home. You can behave that long, can't you?"

I remembered what he'd said about there being a window in Okie's bedroom that could be opened. The bedroom was beyond the kitchen; through the doorway I saw an unmade bed and guessed that Dan had slept in there last night after they'd called Mr. Foster.

Jeremy wasn't looking toward the bedroom. He'd spotted the television on the counter, and a couple of game cartridges alongside it. "Can we play games? Do you have Donkey Kong?"

"You gotta go back upstairs," Dan said, but he didn't sound very firm about it. He was probably as bored as we were.

"Let's play Donkey Kong. Or Road Racing."

Dan hesitated. "Well, I'll have to bring the dogs back in. And when we hear Henry or Pa coming, you high tail it back upstairs."

The Dobermans came when he whistled at them, looking expectantly at the empty dishes beside the stove. While Dan was scooping dog food out of the bag that stood beside them, Shana reached over and took the crusts from Jeremy's hamburger. She dangled them in the air, and one of the dogs reached up and took them out of her hand.

There were still two hamburgers in the sack. Dan wasn't looking, so I unwrapped one, then the other, and shoved them toward Shana. Without any change of expression, she dropped them under the table. They only lasted a matter of seconds.

Dan put the scoop back into the dog food bag and stared at the dogs. "Well, what's the matter with you? I thought you were so all-fired hungry a minute ago."

The dogs, however, only sniffed at the food he'd put out, then dropped flat near Shana's chair, waiting for something else. I thought sure Dan would catch on, but he didn't.

Jeremy and Dan started to play a video game. I could hardly keep my eyes off the telephone; if I could get through to the police, or my folks, we'd soon be out of this place. But though Dan had part of his attention on the game, he didn't turn his back on me. I didn't have a chance to do anything.

Jeremy won two games. Obviously he played a lot. Melissa slid off her chair and put the dish containing the remains of her cereal on the floor, so the dogs could finish it. Dan, who was getting beaten the third game, too, didn't notice when Shana's bowl was set beside Melissa's.

I wasn't quite as afraid of the dogs as I had been. They watched me move around the kitchen, clearing the table, not trying to stop me. They weren't as hostile toward the kids as they had been, either. That might come in handy if we tried to run, though I supposed I couldn't count on it.

I cleared my throat. "When is Mr. Foster going to bring the money?"

"After dark," Dan said. "Boy, kid, you must get a lot of practice at this. Let's try Road Racing."

I could tell by the funny little half-smile on Jeremy's lips that he was pretty good at Road Racing, too. If he kept Dan thinking about video games, was there anything I could do that would help us?

"I hafta go potty," Shana said.

Dan didn't take his attention off the game, because Jeremy was good enough that Dan had to concentrate to hold his own.

I thought of the bathroom upstairs and figured there had to be another one down here; if the old caretaker had been using the upstairs one, there would have been more supplies in it. "Can I take her down here?" I asked, and Dan nodded, jerking a thumb over his shoulder.

"In there," he said.

I was going to wear my heart out, making it hammer so hard. I took Shana into the little hallway off the kitchen. Okie's bedroom I'd already seen into. But hidden from the kitchen was the door to a tiny bathroom, just as old-fashioned as the one upstairs. The window was too small for anybody but Shana to fit through. There was no help there. When we came out, however, I saw that Dan and Jeremy were neck and neck with the Road Racing, and I took a chance.

"Wait here," I whispered to Shana, and I ducked into Okie's bedroom.

The window opened easily. It was big enough for me to go through it, and it was only about six feet off the ground. My chest hurt and I almost forgot to breathe, trying to figure out what to do.

I could get out, all right, but what would I do then? If there had been a close neighbor I might have taken a chance and run, trying that little gate we'd seen from the attic, but the nearest house was a mile or more away. And if they caught me before I got help, we'd be in worse shape than we already were.

I came out of the bedroom and took Shana's hand as we walked back to the kitchen. I felt even worse than I had before, because now I knew it might be possible to get out of the house, at least. Only I didn't know what would happen to the kids if I left them.

Or to me, if I couldn't get through that little gate! If they turned the dogs loose, they'd find me in minutes.

Still, my mind kept racing furiously as I watched Jeremy win another video game, and Dan doggedly begin the fourth one. Dan wasn't terribly smart, and it might yet be possible to outwit him.

If I was smart enough to do it.

Chapter Twelve

It wasn't bad until Henry showed up. He was wearing coveralls that made it look as if he worked in a service station, and when he came in the kitchen door, taking us by surprise, the dogs leaped to their feet and growled.

Henry jumped backward, bellowing something profane about getting rid of them, and Dan yelled, too. "Sit! Stay!"

The Dobermans obediently sank onto their haunches. Melissa had been frightened by them, and she clung to my hand. Shana didn't appear to have been scared at all, regarding the dogs and Henry with an equal amount of interest.

"It's the coveralls," Dan said. "They're not used to the coveralls."

Henry glared at the animals, stepping warily

around them to reach the telephone. "Once this is over, I'll never wear coveralls again," he said, and dialed a number that he read from a scrap of paper.

"Did something go wrong?" Dan asked nervously. He'd just won his first video game, probably because it was one Jeremy had never played before. I wondered if the old man called Okie had had someone to play them with, or if he'd just entertained himself with them all alone.

Henry finished dialing before he answered. "No, I'm just going to check in with Foster; he wants to be sure we actually have the kids before he pays over the ransom. Hello, Mr. Foster? Did you get the money together?"

His grin toward his brother told us what Mr. Foster had said to that. "Good. Good. Now, you want proof we got your kids; I'll let you talk to the little one."

He bent over and held the phone for Shana. "Talk to your daddy, kid."

Shana brightened. Obviously she liked to talk on the phone. "Hi," she said in a very soft voice. "There's big doggies in the shicken."

Henry jerked the phone away. "That convince you? Here, I'll put the middle one on."

Melissa's voice trembled when she lifted her hands to steady the phone. "Daddy, I want to go home."

Again Henry jerked the phone away. "You hear that? She wants to go home. You deliver that suitcase as scheduled, and you'll have them all back within a couple of hours. Now, listen carefully. You got something to write with? You follow my directions exactly, and you'll get your kids back unharmed. What?"

He didn't like being interrupted by Mr. Foster; he scowled, but after a few seconds he handed the phone to me. "He wants to talk to you. Don't tell him anything about where we are, understand?"

I nodded, my mouth suddenly dry. I wouldn't have been surprised if Mr. Foster had been furious with me, letting his kids be kidnapped when I was supposed to be taking care of them, but he sounded nice. Nice, and very worried.

"Darcy?"

"Yes, sir," I said, almost in a whisper.

"Are you all right? Are the kids all right?"

"Yes, sir," I repeated.

"They haven't mistreated any of you?"

I thought of the tape on the kids' mouths, and the way their wrists had been tied. "Not really. We just—"

Henry put an end to that by taking back the receiver. "That's plenty. You know we got the kids. Now, you write this down. At exactly ten o'clock tonight you take that suitcase full of money and leave your house in the gray Mercedes. Don't call the police, don't take anybody with you. Understand? You drive east out of town, on the main road—"

But we had driven west out of town, I thought, feeling panicky. He'd never find us here if he went in the opposite direction . . .

Henry's instructions continued, read off from another paper he'd taken from his pocket. "There's a pay phone two miles out of town, on a Union Station lot. You should be there by ten fifteen. Wait there until we call, and then you'll get further directions. We'll be watching you, so do just what we say."

"I want to go home!" Melissa cried, near tears; and Henry shot an angry look at her.

"Shut her up, or I will," he told me; and I hugged the little girl and murmured something soothing. I'd rather have yelled out where we were, if I'd known how to do it in just a few words.

Henry finally hung up and glared at his brother. "How come they're all down here?"

"They needed something to eat," Dan told him. "What difference does it make? Nobody got away."

Henry looked at the game on the TV set; Jeremy was still holding his set of controls. "Playing games, are you? Having fun?" He sounded angry.

"There's nothing else to do," Dan said sullenly. "And they behave better if they have something to do."

"Who cares how they behave? There's nobody to hear them. Come out and take a look at my car after you lock them up; it's sputtering, threatening to stall, and the last thing we need is a car that quits in the middle of the operation."

Shana spoke up as if there were no serious conversation going on. "I want a jelly butter sandwich."

It was only midmorning, but I guess little kids get hungry fairly often. "If there's peanut butter and bread and jelly, I'll make it for her," I said quickly.

Dan hesitated. "I'll look at the car. You keep an eye on things here," he said; and as he started out the door, Henry spoke sharply.

"Take the dogs out with you."

The Dobermans seemed happy to go, and Henry looked less tense when they'd left the kitchen. I made Shana's sandwich, and on impulse an additional one for each of the rest of us, while Henry carried on a low-voiced conversation on the telephone. I wasn't sure, but I guessed he was talking to his father.

Probably to make sure I didn't make out what he was saying, he turned his back to me. I saw Jeremy walk casually over to the dog food bag and start putting handfuls of it into his pockets. When he caught my eye, he grinned a little, and I nodded. Jeremy had the same idea I did. I made an extra sandwich, just for the dogs, in case I needed to eat my own, though I wasn't the least bit hungry yet.

Henry suddenly turned around to face us.

"Go on back upstairs," he commanded. We did, and it was a relief to get out of the same room with him.

I heard Dan coming back inside. "It was a clogged fuel line. I blew it out," he said.

"Good. Now put those wild animals back on guard duty," Henry ordered, and Dan and the dogs followed us up the stairs.

Once Dan had gone, I tried out my plan. So far nobody but Shana had fed the dogs from her hand, but they'd certainly responded to her. Maybe the rest of us could win them over, too. Maybe they weren't trained guard dogs who'd been taught not to touch food unless it came from their master. Maybe they were just mean-looking dogs that the old man, Okie, had kept for company as well as to frighten prowlers away.

As usual, Shana left her crusts, eating out the middle of her sandwich. When she'd finished the good part, she tore the scraps in half. I wasn't worried about her walking up to the dogs this time, because I was pretty sure they wouldn't hurt her, at least not if she didn't try to go past them.

She dropped a half-circle of crust before each of them, which they caught and swallowed almost instantly.

I decided I didn't need either of the sandwiches I'd carried up, wrapped in paper towels. I stood in the doorway for a moment, gathering my courage, a sandwich in each hand.

"Good dogs," I said uncertainly.

The dogs lay with ears pricked, heads alert, watching. They didn't growl.

That made a me a bit braver. "You want something to eat?" I said, using a soft voice I hoped was disarming. "You like jelly butter sandwiches?"

They didn't wag their tails, nor move, except that their noses quivered.

I took a couple of steps, carefully, so that I wouldn't startle them. I held out the sandwiches. "You want some?"

Behind me, Jeremy said unexpectedly. "Come!"

To my astonishment, both dogs rose to their feet and took a few stiff-legged steps toward us.

"Sit!" Jeremy ordered, and the dogs sat.

Excitement began to build within me. The dogs had been the companions of an old man, and though they'd seen Dan and Henry when they'd worked on the grounds of the estate, they didn't seem to like them particularly. If they'd been pets of Okie's, they might be coaxed into liking someone else who fed them. Neither of the Hazens petted them, or spoke to them except to give orders. And if the dogs would obey Jeremy's orders . . .

I remembered a dog we'd had when I was little, old Foxie. Foxie had done tricks that Tim taught her. "Speak," I requested, and then jumped backward when they each emitted a sharp, single bark.

Quickly, I tossed each of them a full sandwich; they ate them as quickly as they'd eaten the hamburgers earlier that morning.

Downstairs, I heard Henry's voice. "What's going on? What're those kids doing? The dogs barked."

"The kids probably got too close to 'em," Dan said. He'd come to the foot of the stairway, and I moved hastily back into the bedroom. "The dogs are doing just what they're supposed to do."

It seemed as if the dogs should be full by that time, but after the Hazens returned to the kitchen, they continued to watch us hopefully. Jeremy put a hand into a pocket and slowly drew out a few chunks of the dog food.

"Don't make them speak again," I warned him, but he was already edging forward, extending his hand.

"Here, one for each of you," he said, and dropped the food before them.

Better and better, I thought, my excitement continuing to build. If we won over the dogs, we had a brighter chance of getting out of here.

"I wish I'd got to talk to Daddy," Jeremy said. "I'd have told him to come and get us."

"They wouldn't have let you," I assured him. "Don't feed them any more now, wait until later. Maybe they'll let us out of here. If we're lucky, it may be only Dan who stays here while the others are out watching your father and collecting the ransom money. Maybe you can get him to play video games again, so he won't pay so much attention to the rest of us."

"Are we going to escape?" Jeremy demanded.

"I don't know. Maybe we'll try, but you mustn't

say anything to make them suspicious," I warned. "Don't let them know the dogs are beginning to trust us because we're feeding them. Come on, let's read some books for a while, to make the time pass faster."

"Let's go up to the little playroom," Melissa suggested.

"No. Not now. It'll be better if they don't know we've been up there," I said, though I wasn't really certain why it should matter. It might make us look too adventurous, and I wanted them to think they had us too scared to think.

So the day passed slowly, ever so slowly. I thought about Mr. Foster and a suitcase full of money, and for the first time I realized that the Hazens were asking for a fortune. I didn't know the exact amount, but it was surely a lot of money. It wouldn't be right for them to get away with it.

The only good thing I could see coming out of it was that if they took the money and ran off to Mexico, they'd probably go without Diana, if nobody'd found her by now. I didn't think her mother would be mean to her; if her father and brothers were gone, she'd be safe right here at home. I was glad for Diana, if she could stay hidden long enough; there wasn't yet a reason to be glad for the rest of us.

By late afternoon I'd run out of games to play and songs to sing, and my voice was hoarse from reading. Shana had fallen asleep on the mattress, and the other two were playing a game with some pictures I'd torn out of the magazines, when I heard the dogs growl.

Instantly alert, my heart in my throat, I waited. I didn't have to wait very long.

Pa Hazen's voice came from the foot of the stairs. "Come here and call off those blamed dogs! Whose side are they on, anyway?"

"Okie's side, I reckon," Dan told him. "They never been around anybody but Okie and that granddaughter of his that was here a few weeks ago. They don't like strangers. Why don't you just stay away from those kids, Pa? I'll check, but I know they're still up there. They can't get past the dogs. You see how mean they are."

Pa Hazen muttered what he thought of the

dogs, but he didn't come upstairs. It was Dan who appeared.

"I'm hungry," Shana informed him, rubbing her eyes. The conversation had awakened her. She was adjusting to being kidnapped pretty well, I thought. Better than I was. I kept wondering if they would really let me go, when I could tell the police who they were. We were a long way from Mexico, and if the police knew which direction they were heading, they could stop them before they reached the border.

It gave me chills, thinking what the Hazens might do to prevent my telling anybody anything. I tried not to think about it.

"I'm hungry, too," Melissa said. She wasn't as brave as Shana, though. She hung onto my hand whenever she spoke to our captors, as if she thought I could protect her, at least a little bit.

"I'm going out for food right now," Dan told her. "I'll bring back something in about half an hour."

As he turned and started down, Henry called to him. "The car's still spluttering. If you're sure it's the fuel filter, maybe you'd better bring back a new one. You can change it before I leave tonight."

I was glad when they'd all left us alone. The time was coming close, now, when we'd either be rescued, have to escape, or . . . whatever else was going to happen.

I didn't want to think about what that might be, so I concentrated on something else.

"Sit," I said softly to the dogs, and they obeyed. Had they played with Okie's granddaughter when she came to visit? Was that why they liked Shana? Because they'd learned to like another little girl?

"Roll over," Jeremy commanded, and the dogs rolled over.

Even Melissa got into it. "Down," she said, and the Dobermans sank to the floor and rested their heads on their front paws.

Would they let me past them? I wondered, if I offered them a few more bits of dog food? Or would trying set them to barking and give away the fact that I wasn't as docile as I seemed to the Hazens?

It was too early to try anything. Dan had gone

off to town, but Henry and Pa Hazen, who struck me as much more dangerous, were in the house. I could hear their voices from time to time, though I couldn't make out what they said.

I'd hoped they'd let us go downstairs to eat again, but they didn't. Dan brought us a big red and white tub of fried chicken; it was only half-full, so I guessed the others had taken a share of it for themselves. There was cole slaw—none of the kids would touch it, and the dogs didn't want what I didn't eat, either—and potato salad and rolls.

We ate what we wanted, while the dogs watched us. I didn't want to give them chicken bones, but we gave them some skin and the remains of the rolls and a little bit of potato salad.

This time, I dished it out to them myself instead of letting Shana do it. They accepted me as if I'd been feeding them for some time, and gradually my hopes climbed.

Jeremy leaned over and asked me in a loud whisper, "When are we going to escape, Darcy? If we get away soon enough, Daddy won't have to give them the money, will he?"

"I don't know if we can get away that soon," I told him. "Let's all be quiet for a while, now. I want to hear the car when it leaves, all right?"

Jeremy rose and went to the window, pressing his face against it. "I can see it. I can tell you when it leaves."

"It may not leave until after dark. But if it does, let me know. When there's only Dan in the house—" I prayed that there would be a time when it was only Dan we'd have to contend with. "—maybe we'll have a chance."

And at last the time came. It was just barely dark, and Shana had fallen asleep on the mattress; Melissa was nearly asleep, too. I was amazed at Jeremy's patience, standing looking downward into the side yard; and then he turned, speaking again in that loud whisper that could possibly have been understood out in the hallway.

"The car's driving away!"

"Could you see who got into it?"

"Two men," Jeremy said readily. "I think it's Dan still here. Now can we escape?"

My breathing was suddenly very fast. "Now

we see if I can get past the dogs. You stay here and look after the girls, okay?"

His lower lip came out in a pout, the way Shana's sometimes did. "I want to go, too. They're asleep, so we'll have to come back after them if we find a way out, won't we? So why can't I come, too? I'll be real quiet, honest I will."

I looked at him, afraid and uncertain, knowing that if I did the wrong thing this time, it was possible that none of us would ever get home again.

"Well, let me see first if the dogs will let me past. Give me a little bit of the dog food."

He handed it over, and feeling as if my heart was in my mouth, I took a few cautious steps toward the two huge dogs at the top of the stairs.

Chapter Thirteen

The dogs didn't move, and they didn't growl as I approached. I spoke softly to them, while they kept their ears pricked up and waited.

I hoped I wasn't making a mistake, putting out a hand very slowly with the dog food on it, because if I was, it would be a *big* mistake. I had to try it, though. If the dogs wouldn't allow me down those stairs, I didn't see what I could possibly do to get us out of this mess.

The nearest dog turned his head slightly toward me as I moved my hand within a couple of inches of his nose—and those sharp teeth— and held it there. "You want some?" I asked, almost in a whisper.

For a few seconds nothing happened, and then the dog stretched his neck and sniffed my hand.

"Go ahead," I told him, "take it."

It was a very peculiar feeling when his tongue touched my palm, and then the dog food was gone. I still had my fingers, I thought, elated, and tried the same thing with the other dog.

"I'm going to go downstairs," I told them in that same quiet voice. "And you're going to stay here and guard Melissa and Shana. All right? Guard?"

They seemed to know that word. Their tails twitched ever so slightly.

"I'm going, too," Jeremy said. He, too, spoke very softly. He offered more bits of food; and then, when they'd accepted it, he put out a hand and stroked first one dark head, then the other. The dogs twitched their tails again.

And they let us walk between them, turning their heads to watch us.

"Stay," I said. "Guard," and Jeremy echoed my words.

We crept down the stairway, lighted only from above; when we reached the bottom and the front entryway, it was pretty dark, though there was a light in the kitchen at the rear of the house, as before.

I tried the front door again, found it locked as expected, and put a finger on my lips to warn Jeremy to silence. Then we edged toward that lighted doorway.

The TV was on, and Dan sat at the table, absorbed in what sounded like a cops and robbers show. The telephone was out of sight to our left; the door to the bedroom was out of sight to our right.

"What are we going to do?" Jeremy whispered.

I swallowed hard. "There's a window in Okie's bedroom that opens. We need to get in there. Maybe, when the show's in an exciting part, we could crawl on our hands and knees, and he wouldn't see us. His back's this direction, anyway, and if we don't bump into anything, or make any noise, he might not notice us."

"Okay," Jeremy said, moving forward, and I caught his shoulder.

"No, wait until there's a chase or a gun fight, or something that really holds his attention." I had to decide which way to do it. "I'll tell you when, and you get into the bedroom and wait for me, out of sight. I'll follow as soon as I can."

We dropped to hands and knees and crept closer to where the light spilled out into the hallway. Dan was eating a sandwich and had a can of pop before him, his eyes were practically glued to the screen.

Suddenly sirens went off and he leaned forward, forgetting to chew.

"Now!" I whispered, and Jeremy scuttled forward.

It seemed to me that he went very slowly, though he didn't make a sound. My chest hurt from holding my breath. And then Jeremy vanished from sight, and Dan was still watching the screen. I was just about to follow after Jeremy when Dan suddenly stood up and went to the refrigerator for another can of pop. If he'd been facing the doorway, he'd have seen me for sure; but he didn't notice a thing, sinking back into his chair and popping the top of the can.

The sound of gunfire replaced the sirens. I closed my eyes, breathed a small prayer, and started forward.

After the first few seconds, I didn't look at Dan. I crawled across the corner of the kitchen and had to restrain myself from making a dive for the shadowed bedroom. I was wet with sweat and felt as if I might be shot from behind at any minute, though I hadn't seen any of the Hazens with guns.

"The window's open," Jeremy said in my ear. It was a wonder I heard him, the way the blood was pounding in my head.

"Okay. This time I'll go first, because it's a ways down," I told him. "Then I'll catch you when you jump out."

It was as easy as that. I jumped, making no more than a dull thud as I hit the ground, and then Jeremy came into my arms. He was heavy enough so I staggered backward, but I didn't fall down.

Only then, looking back up the rectangle lighted by what illumination filtered through from the kitchen, did it occur to me that it might be harder to get back in, if we had to, than it had been to get out. I hoped Shana and Melissa wouldn't wake up and be frightened to find us gone.

There was no point in worrying about getting back in the house until we had to. Though it had seemed quite dark, after a few minutes our eyes adjusted, and we could see well enough to move around without bumping into the trees. I stood for a moment, getting my bearings.

"The little gate's over that way," Jeremy told me, and I thought he was right. If only it would be unlocked!

A tiny beam of light pierced the darkness, and I yelped before I realized that Jeremy had a tiny flashlight. "I found it on the table by the bed in Okie's room," he said.

"Keep it turned away from the house," I told him. "It'll sure make this easier." We set off in the direction of the small gate we'd seen from the cupola.

It was so well hidden that it took us a while to find it. It had been plain enough, seen from above, but from the ground, and at night, it seemed impossible to locate. I tried to recall what we'd seen, and finally remembered that there'd been a big tree just to the left of it. The yard was full of trees, but we kept looking just to the *right* of all those close to the wall, and at last we found the gate.

I got scratched, pushing aside the shrubbery to reach it. It was much smaller than the one we'd driven through, made of wrought iron in a fancy pattern, and it stood ajar. Hope made me giddy, until I tried to push it further open—or pull it, whichever way it would go.

It wouldn't move at all. It had apparently stood open for years, and some of the shrubs had grown through it, around it, wedging it into its present position. Beyond it, the shrubs outside the wall seemed even thicker than on this side.

"I can't get through it," I said helplessly, disappointment making my chest ache. "It won't move."

"Maybe I can," Jeremy suggested. He pushed forward through the branches; and sure enough, he could just barely squeeze through the opening. However, the shrubs on the other side were almost impossible to go through without scratching him pretty badly. And what would he do, alone, if he came out the other side?

I could see his face in the reflected light of the tiny flashlight. His eyes were big and scared.

"Maybe I can get all the way through," he said. "Only I don't know where to go." His voice quavered a little bit.

"I don't know, either," I told him. "You could follow the wall around that way, to the front where the driveway comes in, and then follow that to the main road, but it's a long way to another house. No, I don't think this is going to work."

"What are we going to do, then?" Jeremy asked. I think he was more disappointed than I was; we'd counted on finding a way off the grounds once we were free of the house.

I didn't know for sure what time it was, probably nine o'clock or maybe even a little later. At ten Mr. Foster would leave the house with the money. The kidnappers were going to make him run around from place to place, stopping in various phone booths for instructions. I didn't know how long that would take, but it would be nerve wracking for the Hazens as well as for Jeremy's father. I didn't think they'd keep it up for hours.

Before long, they'd be back here with the money. They'd have made sure the police weren't following Mr. Foster or watching them. And then—maybe they'd let the kids go. Maybe.

I couldn't count on them doing the same with me. And possibly they wouldn't even leave the kids where someone would find them. If they'd paid any attention to Jeremy, they might realize that he could describe them as well as I could, and that he'd overheard their names, too. Jeremy was smart for six.

"What're we going to do?" Jeremy repeated.

And it was then, out of the depths of despair, that I got the marvelous idea.

Chapter Fourteen

"Can't we escape then?" Jeremy asked, and he sounded as if he were going to cry.

"Not this way. But maybe I've thought of something better," I told him, reaching for his hand. "Come on, let's go back to the house."

"What's better than escaping? I don't want to go in the house; I don't like them, not even Dan. He cheats."

"That doesn't surprise me. Well, maybe we'll cheat a little, too, only in a different way. It's not really cheating if you're trying to save your own lives," I reasoned aloud.

"What are we going to do?" he demanded, trotting to keep up with me.

I stopped. "Wait. Give me the flashlight. Come on back to the little gate."

"I thought we couldn't fit through it," Jeremy

protested, though he came along willingly enough.

"We can't," I said, "but maybe we can make the kidnappers *think* we got out that way."

He was so astonished he forgot to walk. "What good'll that do?"

"It might make them scared that we'll get somewhere and call the police. It might make them decide not to meet your father and take the ransom money, for fear they'll get caught doing it and go to jail for a long time. It might make them run away and leave the front gate unlocked and the telephone unguarded, so we can really get rescued."

I had taken the little flashlight and played its beam on the shrubbery around the small gate. The first thing to do, I decided, was to make it visible, show them where we might have gone. I handed the light to him and told him where to point it, then began to break off branches and trample them down.

"I want them to see our trail," I explained to Jeremy. "It would help if we could break down some branches on the other side of the wall, too, only I can't reach very many. Maybe if I tear a piece out of my shirt, so they'll think I've squeezed through . . ."

My shirt, though, was no more easily torn than the blanket I'd thought of converting to a rope. It wouldn't tear at all, and neither would my jeans.

"Maybe my shirt," Jeremy suggested. He was wearing a knit pullover in bold brown, white, and bright yellow stripes.

"Let's try it," I agreed. "Yellow would show up the best, if they're looking around in the dark." We lifted his shirt, fixed a wide yellow stripe over one of the projections on the gate, and I pulled down as hard as I could. All it did was punch a hole in a perfectly good shirt.

"I could tear it now, I think," Jeremy said, and stuck his finger in the hole and pulled.

It took a couple of tries, but we got a small bit of fabric off and we stuck it on the fence, like a tiny flag.

"Shall we leave a white stripe, too?" Jeremy asked, really getting into the spirit of things.

"No. I think that might be overkill," I told him, and then had to explain what that meant.

"Have you got any dog food left?" I asked then.

"About a handful," Jeremy answered, showing me.

"Okay. Put it here on the ground, in front of the gate. It might make the dogs come here so the men'll see the scrap of your shirt. Dump out all you have left," I said, and he did.

When we'd done all we could to make it seem we'd escaped through the small gate, we headed for the house.

Through the kitchen window we could see Dan, still watching television. So all we had to do was get inside, get past him and back upstairs. I looked around for something to climb on to reach the opened window, and Jeremy tugged at my arm.

"Darcy, if we aren't really going to escape, what are we going to do?"

"We're going to hide," I said with the first satisfaction I'd felt in quite a while. "Here, if I move this garbage can over and boost you up, can you crawl through the window? Be sure to be real quiet."

The first try we tipped over the can and the

lid came off. My heart was in my throat for fear it had made enough noise to attract Dan's attention; but when I checked, he was still glued to the TV. I wondered how he stayed so thin when he ate so much; now he was eating a Hershey Big Block bar.

We set the garbage can back up, and this time we both made it into Okie's bedroom. I could hardly believe that Dan would sit there, so engrossed in violence and action on the screen that he wouldn't know we were creeping around behind him, but he did.

We were scared, though. Again Jeremy went first and I followed. Just as I was right behind him, Dan suddenly pushed back his chair from the table; and for the second time in just a little while, I thought my heart would stop.

Dan didn't get up, though. He only leaned back and put his feet up on another chair; after a few seconds I started to crawl and got out of sight. I would have simply collapsed there in the dim hallway until my breathing was normal again if I'd dared, only I didn't.

We got up and moved quickly through the dark hall. At the foot of the stairs I paused, heard the TV going full blast in the kitchen, and called softly to the dogs.

"We're coming up, and don't bark, okay? Stay."

The Dobermans regarded us with no more than friendly interest as we climbed the stairs. This time I was brave enough to pat each of them on the head, and even to scratch behind their ears. "Good dogs," I said to them, and was rewarded by two wagging rear ends.

I stepped to the doorway of the bedroom, where the light made a yellow rectangle on the floor. The little girls were sleeping soundly, Shana on her stomach with her long hair hanging over the edge of the mattress onto the floor, Melissa spreadeagled on her back.

"Darcy," Jeremy said, and I turned around to look at him. "Where are we going to hide?"

"In the cupola," I told him. "I don't think the Hazens even know it's there, and that mattress practically covers up the door when it leans against the wall. I think we could stand it up so we could crawl in behind it, and nobody'd notice a thing." If we're lucky, I added silently, but at least we were trying to do something. I didn't see how my plan could make things any worse than they already were.

Jeremy's eyes were bright. "Are we going up there now?"

"As soon as we can. We'll have to have something to sleep on. We can't take the mattress—in fact, I don't think we could get a mattress through that little door and up those narrow stairs; but we'll take the blanket, and maybe some of the clothes out of those trunks. Come on. The sooner we get settled, the better."

It took a while. Jeremy was very helpful; he rummaged through the trunks in the attic and came up with a rug, two ragged old sleeping bags, and a couple more blankets. They smelled funny, but I figured that was the least of our problems.

We made beds on the floor of the cupola room, then decided what else we needed. We took the box of books up, because we didn't know how long we'd be there. And water. We'd need water. We had trouble finding something to carry it in, and finally rinsed out some old canning jars and filled them. Then we looked around for something to use when Shana had to go to the bathroom. It was Jeremy who located that item, too, bringing it to me from a far corner of the attic with a self-satisfied grin. "Look! A potty chair!" he said, and carried it up to our hiding place, smearing dust all over his front as he went.

The dogs watched us with apparent interest, making no objection to our running around, or to my carrying the sleeping girls up to the attic when everything was ready. Shana slept all the way to the top; but I had to wake Melissa up so she could walk the final flight, because there wasn't room enough for me to carry her on those narrow, twisting steps.

I'd have liked to lurk downstairs and listen for the phone to ring—hoping I'd be able to interpret one end of the conversation when Dan answered—or for someone to come with news. Only when I suggested leaving the kids alone, Jeremy turned uncooperative.

"I don't want you to go," he said, and the quaver was back in his voice.

"Okay," I agreed. "Come on, we'll try to get some rest so we'll be ready for action when it's time, all right?"

He fell asleep almost as soon as he stretched out on the sleeping bag beside Shana. At least I thought he had. It was a warm night, and I left the windows open. I could hear crickets somewhere, and bullfrogs. Was there a pond nearby? Even if I got to use the phone, I didn't know how to tell them where we were. Maybe if I gave them the phone number, the police could trace that. Yes, that was the thing to do, I decided.

"Darcy?"

I turned toward the small voice. "Yes, Jeremy. I'm here."

"I hate those men. I hope the police lock them up."

"I hope so too," I said, reaching out a hand to touch his. "They probably will."

There was a minute or so of silence, and then he spoke again, sounding very sleepy, "I wish those bees would sting them and sting them, and then the police would come."

I squeezed his hand once more, and before long I could tell by his breathing that he'd really fallen asleep this time.

I wanted to sleep, too, but I didn't. I sat

there in the darkness, listening to the frogs and the crickets, wishing I knew what was going on. Mr. Foster might have delivered the ransom money by now. Was there any chance he'd told the police, and they'd been smart enough to watch and follow and catch the kidnappers? Or had the Hazens gotten away with it, and were they headed back here?

I sat there thinking and thinking, and pretty soon another idea had jelled in my head.

It was an idea that gave me goosebumps, but it wouldn't go away. It was Jeremy's idea, really, but now it was mine, too.

I'm afraid of bees or wasps or hornets, or anything else that stings or bites. But I was more afraid of what the kidnappers would do before they headed for Mexico with the ransom money, if the police hadn't been able to stop them.

My mouth got dryer, and I kept thinking about those wasps. After a while, I knew I had to do it, no matter how much it scared me.

Chapter Fifteen

Even after I decided I had to do it, I continued to sit there in the dark, thinking about it.

I remembered very clearly the day that Tim had knocked a wasp nest off our garage; the angry creatures had swarmed all over, stinging everyone in sight. I got stung twice, which was less than Tim and Jimmy and Bobby got. One place was on my leg, and that was bad enough, but the second sting was far worse.

There were wasps flying around my head, and I was terrified that they were going to get tangled up in my hair; I ran for the house, waving my arms to chase them away. One of them landed on my thumb, and I yelped and brushed it off with my other hand, but not before it stung me.

I could still remember how much it hurt.

The pain wasn't just in my thumb, either; it traveled all the way up my arm to my shoulder, and it ached so bad I couldn't sleep that night. It was a couple of days before it stopped hurting, no matter what Mom put on the sting to draw the poison out. Dad said the stinger must have gone into a nerve and followed it up, and that was why it made my whole arm and shoulder hurt. Tim said that wasps and bees had the same poison as rattlesnakes, and that's why they were so painful. I didn't know if that was true or not, but I hoped never to get bitten by a rattler.

I hadn't had anything to do with knocking that nest down. In fact, I'd yelled at Tim to leave it alone.

And now I was thinking about taking down another one, because it was the only weapon I could think of that I could use to protect us from a trio of kidnappers.

I wasn't sure how I could manage to use it against the Hazens and still protect the kids and myself, yet there wasn't anything else.

Nothing at all.

Pretty soon I got up and went over to the

window. With the little flashlight I could see the papery nest, like an out-of-shape balloon, right there under the eaves. It would be easy to get to, just by putting one foot through the window opening, straddling the frame, and reaching up for it. It wasn't high or hard to reach.

Tim told me that bees and wasps don't move around at night. They're inside their nest, and quiet. I get a lot of my information from Tim, and most of it's accurate, though not all of it. I hoped he was right about night being the safest time to try to do something with wasps.

I couldn't just tear the nest down and leave it sitting around until I found the right use for it, of course. I had a nasty suspicion that the wasps would wake up and defend themselves the minute the nest pulled away from the eaves; for all I knew, there would be a hole in the top of it when it came loose, so the whole swarm could fly out at once.

I ducked my head out the window, and I could hear them, buzzing ever so faintly. So they weren't even asleep, or maybe they made, that noise all the time.

I couldn't tear the nest down, I thought. It

would practically be suicide, unless I had something to put it in to make sure the wasps didn't start stinging until I wanted them to, and I didn't have anything like that.

In the trash downstairs, left over from our fast food chicken dinner, there was a plastic bag the rolls had come in. It was quite a big bag; obviously Dan had bought enough rolls to feed them as well as us.

Was it big enough to put over the wasp nest before I tore it loose from the eaves?

I sighed very softly. I'd have to find out.

The kids were sleeping peacefully. I took the little flashlight and started down the stairway, stooping at the bottom to crawl through the small doorway, which was even more cramped now that the mattress was leaned over it again.

I went through the attic, down the other flight of stairs, and opened the door at the bottom. The light was still on, the dogs were still lying at the top of the stairs. They lifted their heads and thumped their tails hopefully.

"Sorry, fellas, I don't have anything this time," I said, but I paused to scratch behind their ears, just to keep them remembering that they'd changed sides and were friends of mine now.

The trash was where we'd left it. The plastic bag was wadded up with napkins in it, which I emptied out into the cardboard chicken bucket. I thought it looked big enough.

There was a lump growing in my throat. I folded up the plastic bag, and then I heard the car coming.

It was quite a way off, but the only car I'd heard since we were brought here was the one the Hazens were driving. I felt paralyzed, suffocating. The night was suddenly not warm but hot.

I stood by the window that overlooked the side yard, listening. The car came closer, and then it stopped—someone was opening the gate—and after a minute the headlights came through the trees, and the car rolled to a halt below me.

The screen door slammed, and Dan called out hoarsely. "That you, Henry? Pa?"

"Who else you think it would be, you idiot?" Henry said with his usual foul humor. They had turned off only the engine, not the headlights. The two of them got out, and when Pa Hazen came around the front of the car I saw that he was carrying a briefcase or small suitcase.

"You get it?" Dan asked eagerly, and again he was snarled at.

"We got it, we got it, now let's get out of here. I told your ma we was all going fishing over the weekend, so she won't start looking for us before Sunday night. We can get a long way off by then."

"Is it all there? As much as we asked for?" Dan demanded.

"Far as we can tell. We didn't stop to count it," his brother replied sarcastically.

"Aren't we gonna leave any of it for Ma and the girls?"

"Sure, so the minute she spends it suspicion points at us?" The sarcasm was even heavier. "You can bet they marked the bills, even if we did tell 'em not to. Can't you get it through your head that we gotta be careful until we're out of the country?"

Pa Hazen cut through Henry's voice. "Go on, get in the car. I'll go take care of the kids."

Dan had sounded jubilant. Now he sounded uneasy. "What do you mean, take care of them? You're going to give them back to their folks, aren't you? Now that they paid the ransom?"

"Don't worry about that, get your stuff and get in the car. I'll be back in a few minutes," Pa Hazen said.

Though the breeze drifting through the open window was warm, goosebumps rose on my arms.

I was certain—*absolutely certain*—that Pa Hazen didn't intend to take us all home, maybe not even the kids.

The screen door slammed again, and Dan swore. "Listen, I told you both, I wasn't getting mixed up in anything more than just holding the kids for ransom. You said we'd take 'em home as soon as we had the money—"

I turned away from the window, only now realizing that if I'd been downstairs when Dan went out, I'd have had time to call the police while there was no one in the kitchen. If only that had occurred to me earlier—

It hadn't, and in a minute Pa Hazen would be coming, and I had to be gone.

I'd no more than closed the door at the foot of the attic stairs when I heard him coming. I heard the dogs growl, and he cursed them, and then he bellowed in rage. I thought he was yelling out the window at his sons below, but I heard his words, all right.

My mom would have washed anybody's mouth out with soap for using the kind of words he was yelling. The gist of it was that we were gone, and the dogs had let us go. Miss Jacobson would have flunked him in grammar, but he knew more cuss words than I'd ever heard before.

I cowered there on the stairs, torn between fleeing to the cupola and fear that I'd be overheard if I moved.

And then there was a *thunk* that I figured out a little later must have been Pa Hazen kicking one of the dogs.

It was a mistake.

The racket on the other side of the door from me was incredible. Snarling, growling, barking—and Pa Hazen yelling bloody murder, sounding as if he were really hurt.

"Good dogs," I muttered; and under cover of

all the fury behind me, I started up the stairs to the attic. I heard running feet, and Dan yelling at the dogs; and then things quieted down somewhat, though Pa Hazen continued to swear. I paused at the top of the climb to catch my breath and heard Dan say, "You shouldn't of messed with the dogs, Pa! You must of been crazy to *kick* one of 'em when you knew they didn't like you in the first place!"

"I need a doctor! Look what he done to my leg! It needs to be sewed up before I bleed to death!"

Henry had come at the sound of trouble, too. "We can't take you to a doctor, Pa, not here in town. I'm pretty sure they have to report dog bites to the cops, and they might put two and two together before we've had time to get out of the country. The old man's got a medicine chest downstairs; we'll put disinfectant on it and fix you up with tape and bandages, at least until we get to some other town far enough away so the local cops won't hear about it. What happened to the kids?"

There was more profanity. "—Dogs nearly took my leg off, but they didn't stop the kids!

Where are they? You were supposed to be watching 'em!"

"I couldn't watch every minute, could I? They must be here somewhere; they couldn't of got by me in the kitchen, and that was the only way out," Dan said aggrievedly.

"Well, you tell me where they went," Pa Hazen said. "Help me down them stairs, I'm bleedin' like a stuck pig."

"Dan can take you. I'll find the kids," Henry said, and his tone made my blood run even colder than it already was.

I couldn't stay there any longer. He'd check the other bedrooms first, and then he'd investigate the attic. I had to be up in that cupola before he came.

I was grateful for the little flashlight Jeremy had found; I'd have broken my neck getting across the attic and advertised my whereabouts to Henry, now that his father had gone downstairs to continue his yelling.

I crawled behind the mattress, eased open the door, and immediately I heard Jeremy's frightened voice.

"Darcy?"

"Yes, it's me. Stay there." I shined the light upward and caught his scared face.

"What's happening? I heard the dogs and woke up, and you were gone, and I thought—"

I reached him and gave him a reassuring hug. "No, it wasn't me they bit, it was Pa Hazen. Listen, remember what you said about that wasp nest? About wishing the wasps would sting the kidnappers? Well, I went down and got a plastic bag; and if you'll help me maybe we can get the nest into it. If they come near us, maybe we can throw it at them and run for it. Or something."

It took two of us. We were both scared, yet excited, too, as we took the little "shicken" table out onto the barely slanting roof so Jeremy could stand on it to hold the plastic bag in place after I'd eased it over the papery nest. I was shaking, and it was all I could do to make myself touch it, which was necessary because it just barely went into the bag.

"Now, you hold the bag up tight against the roof," I said. We had the flashlight lying on the windowsill; we couldn't aim it at the wasp nest, so it wasn't easy to see what we were doing. I had taken a tiny spatula from the toy dishes in the "shicken," and now I began to pry at the edges of the nest where it was stuck to the eaves.

I could have done it faster if I hadn't been so scared I'd knock a hole in it and set the wasps free. I inched around it from all sides, loosening the nest, until Jeremy said, "Hurry up, Darcy, my arms hurt!"

I sucked in a deep breath. "Okay. Hold it as tight as you can now, and I'll knock it the rest of the way off."

And then the nest came loose; I grabbed the bag, twisted the top, and secured it with the twistem that had come with it.

I was drenched in sweat when I placed the bag and nest on the little table and helped Jeremy down.

He was back inside the cupola, and I had one leg over the bottom of the window ledge, when we heard doors slamming and voices below. I could hear them as plainly as I had from the bedroom below.

"They're not in the house. You must have let them walk right past you or something,"

Henry said, furious. "We gave you the easiest job; even a moron could have done it; and you blew it!"

By now they had flashlights, too. I saw the beams sweep through the trees on that side of the house.

"Here's how they got out, you fool," Pa Hazen said, and I heard the garbage can lid clatter. "They got past you and out the window." It never occurred to them that we could have escaped without the garbage can and could only have moved it under the window after we were out, in order to get back in.

"Then they have to be still on the grounds," Dan said defensively. "The gates were locked. We'll just get the dogs out here, and they'll find them."

"The fool dogs let them go downstairs; what makes you think they'll find them for us?" There was a savagery in Henry that made me glad he'd stopped short of finding the tiny door at the far end of the attic.

"Well, even if the dogs *like* the kids, they'll probably find them," Dan insisted. "Let me call them out here."

"Not with me around," Pa Hazen said, and then the car door slammed.

Dan whistled, and I heard the Dobermans. They went running.

"Find the kids," Dan ordered, and I saw the lights touching the trees again.

It was dark where we were and I didn't dare use my own flashlight, even though they probably weren't looking for us on the roof. But I had to know what was going on. I began to walk very carefully toward the edge of the roof, then dropped down to my hands and knees, feeling very carefully ahead of me before I moved.

"Here!" Dan shouted, and the dogs ran barking enthusiastically toward him, plunging into the shrubbery. "There's another gate here, and it isn't even shut! They must have got out here!"

There was more cursing, and the brothers came back to the car. I couldn't hear what they said then, because they stuck their heads in through the open car windows. I prayed they'd all get in the car and drive away, and then I could use the phone.

Something flickered in the darkness. For a

minute I didn't know what it was. I stared off over the tops of the trees toward the main road.

Lights, familiar lights. Blue, blinking lights.

A police car.

It wasn't very close, but there was a police car out there. Could they have followed the Hazens when they picked up the suitcase with the money? Or were they there for something else entirely?

I moved back a yard or two from the edge of the roof and shined my light at the distant car, but it was too little; I knew that at once.

Did the lights inside the cupola still work? I didn't know, we hadn't tried them, but I called back to Jeremy, who stood at the open window.

"Try the light switch, there at the top of the stairs!"

A moment later light flooded the whole top of the house. There were some excited exclamations from below; but it was too late to worry about the Hazens.

"Flick it off and on," I said, and Jeremy obediently wiggled the switch up and down.

SOS, I thought. Was it three shorts, three

longs, or the other way around? Once you got started, what difference did it make?

The blinking blue lights were still there, though I couldn't tell if they were in the same place or not. If the car was facing this way, a driver couldn't help seeing the beacon of light streaming out from the cupola, could he?

I made a dive for the window, feet skidding momentarily on the gritty roofing, and then I was over the sill, pushing Jeremy's fingers off the light switch. Long, long, long—short, short, short. SOS.

"Oh, help, please help!" I cried.

Melissa sat up, pushing her hair out of her eyes in bewilderment. "What's the matter? Aren't we home yet?"

"Here, Jeremy, keep doing this," I said. "I have to see if that police car is still out there—"

It wasn't.

I stood at the window, disappointment almost bending me double with pain. How could they not have seen the beacon? How could they not have understood the message? Every Scout in the world knows the signal for SOS, doesn't he?

The Hazens were yelling; and then I realized that the voices weren't outside anymore. "There must be a way up from the attic!" Henry hollered, and the door slammed again. Twice.

The police car had gone, and now the kidnappers knew where we were. Jeremy was still flipping the light switch; and in a few minutes they'd find us, and there was no help on the way.

For the first time I thought I'd really cry, only how could I, with Jeremy looking so hopeful, and Melissa so scared, and Shana just waking up, too.

A moment later, we heard men's heavy feet on the attic stairs.

Chapter Sixteen

It would be only a matter of minutes, at most, before the kidnappers found the tiny door behind the mattress. They'd seen our signal lights; they knew we had to be up here.

I'd hoped that if they saw the light they'd take the money and run, leaving us to be rescued. If they were coming after us, instead, I figured it was for one reason, because I saw it that way on TV: they would hold us as hostages, to make sure the police wouldn't shoot at them and keep them from getting away.

The kids were looking to me for help, the fear back in their faces, even Shana's, though I'm sure she didn't know what was happening. She only knew that everyone else was afraid, so she was afraid, too.

The plastic bag was there, and a few of

the wasps had come out of the grayish globe and were crawling around. The rest of them would undoubtedly come out, too, as soon as they could.

I didn't have much time to think. "Come on, out the window, all of you," I ordered. Only Jeremy obeyed, and I picked up first Shana and then Melissa and stuck them through the opening after their brother.

"Don't move around, lie down right there," I instructed. The last thing I wanted was for any of them to get near the edge of the roof. With the lights blazing in the cupola, we could at least see where the edge was, but the kids were so little, Shana hardly more than a baby and still groggy from just waking up.

The men below had found the door to the cupola room. I had only seconds to spare as I slid through the window opening out onto the roof and reached back inside for the plastic bag.

Just as Henry's head appeared at the top of the stairs opposite my window, I turned the plastic bag upside down, inside the room, and tugged the window closed.

Henry had seen me, and he had no idea what I'd just done. He ran toward me, with Dan only a few steps behind him, his rage plain enough on his face to make me shudder.

And then all of a sudden, just as Henry put out his hands to raise the window again, the wasps did what they were supposed to do.

I was terrified of the men, and I guess maybe I hated them, too, for what they'd done and were trying to do. Yet I almost felt sorry for them as the wasps began to sting.

There were a dozen or more of them around Henry's head, landing on his face and his ears, before he understood what was happening.

He took his hands off the window and started yelling and beating at the wasps, which only made them madder than they already were. I hadn't even had time to flop down flat on the roof like the kids—for once they'd obeyed orders immediately, without argument—and I was staring straight into Henry's face as the wasps landed on him, all over every exposed bit of skin.

He screamed and clawed at his eyes, and then he turned and stumbled back down those steep, narrow stairs.

By this time Dan was screaming and crying. He, too, headed almost blindly for the stairs; I heard him fall, still screaming.

Some of the other windows had remained open, so we heard them very plainly. A few wasps darted out into the darkness of the rooftop, but most of them buzzed and spun in the cupola room, seeking their enemies. So far none of them had come anywhere near us; they stayed in the lighted area.

From below, Pa Hazen started to yell. "Hey, what's going on up there? What's happening? Come on, we gotta get out of here!"

I doubt if Henry and Dan heard him. I could imagine them still fighting off the stinging creatures that crawled down their necks and up their sleeves and into their ears.

A new element was added about then, when the dogs began to bark furiously. I thought Pa Hazen had become alarmed enough to get out of the car—which wasn't a wise thing to do, because the Dobermans went after him, from the sound of things.

Jeremy, wide-eyed, was sitting up, tugging at my pants leg. "Darcy, look! Look!"

And when I turned away from the awful sight of the Hazen brothers and the wasps, I saw the most welcome sight in the world.

Coming fairly fast through the woods was a car with spinning blue lights that flickered in and out between the trees.

Things were pretty confusing for a while. Expecting to drive out immediately, the Hazens had closed the gate but not locked it. The police car came through, and before it had stopped in the yard beside the black sedan, I could hear sirens in the distance, and then we saw the lights of more emergency vehicles. There were at least four of them.

"It's the cops!" Jeremy cried. "We're saved, Darcy! We're rescued!"

It wasn't quite as simple as that, because we were on the roof three tall stories above the ground, and we couldn't go back through the cupola room because it was full of wasps, though Henry and Dan were gone. Even if they were in the attic, or downstairs, I didn't think they'd be dangerous anymore.

I dropped to my hands and knees and crept

over to the edge of the roof, staying far enough back to be sure I wouldn't fall. Two uniformed officers had gotten out of the patrol car—between their headlights, the revolving blue lights, and the headlights on the old black sedan, it was light as day down there—and they drew their guns.

Pa Hazen had gotten back into the black sedan and one of the Dobermans was on each side of it, leaping toward the windows, barking and snarling. I made a mental note never to kick a Doberman. Apparently they didn't forget easily.

I yelled when it dawned on me that the officers were going to shoot the dogs. "No! Don't shoot them, they saved our lives! Don't shoot!"

The officers looked up, and another patrol car eased through the gate. "You one of the Foster kids?" one of them called up, and relief flowed through me so strongly that I felt dizzy and pulled back from the edge of the roof.

"I'm the baby-sitter, Darcy Stevens!" I shouted, to make sure they heard me over the sound of the dogs. "Down, boys! Sit! You hear me, sit!"

To everybody's astonishment, including mine, the dogs fell back from the black sedan, their tongues hanging out, their fangs catching the light in great sharp points.

"Good boys," I said. "Good dogs."

"Are the Foster kids with you?" There was a circle of police officers, now, and some other men who weren't in uniform; I thought they were probably police, too. Plain clothes detectives, maybe, or FBI men.

"They're here. We're all right, but we can't get down the way we came up because the cupola is full of wasps. The other two kidnappers got stung, and they went down the stairs," I explained.

"You stay right there, back from the edge," the spokesman told me. "We'll get you down. We'll call for a fire department ladder truck."

So that was how we got off the roof. Firemen carried Jeremy and Melissa and Shana, which Jeremy thought was great fun; and I climbed down by myself. I'd have felt silly being carried, as big as I was. I was glad I was wearing jeans.

The fireman had to put on special clothes

and masks because of the wasps. They didn't have any trouble with Dan and Henry, who came out of the house in a very subdued state and were put into the back of one of the police cars. Pa Hazen was in a different one, yelling to be taken to the hospital.

I decided Tim must be right about the stings being like the venom of a rattlesnake, because those kidnappers were so sick and swollen I wouldn't even have recognized them.

By the time we got down, Clancy was there with the others. He called me over to his own patrol car and stuck a mike in my face. "Here, talk to Mr. Foster."

Mr. Foster kept asking if everybody was all right, and I kept telling him they were. Mrs./Dr. Foster was there at the police station, too, and she sounded as if she were crying. And then they let me talk to my dad, who was there with them. I had to tell it all over again for him, that nobody was hurt except the kidnappers.

After that it got sort of hokey. When we got to town—Jeremy had a terrible time choosing whether to ride in the police cruiser or the fire truck, and finally decided on the cruiser with the rest of us after they told him they couldn't run the siren on the fire truck—everybody'd been crying or started crying all over again, except the Foster kids and me.

"Darcy—" a familiar voice said, and I turned to see Mrs. Murphy extending a hand to touch my shoulder. "My dear child, I'm so glad you're safe. All of you. I was so shocked when I learned that they used my car and my door opener to get into the garage—though it did provide a clue to your whereabouts, I suppose. It was found in a gravel pit, and the police thought whoever had driven it there had left on foot. So they were watching that area while Mr. Foster went to meet the kidnappers with the ransom money, and then they saw your signal. How clever you were, to think of signaling that way."

I felt sort of peculiar. She seemed very nice, but I didn't like the way she'd taken care of the Foster kids. My mom was right, they needed more love and attention than they'd gotten from her while their parents were working. I didn't know what to say to her; and I didn't know if I should discuss it with Mrs./Dr. Foster, either. Mostly my mom taught me to mind my own business, but some things can really get to be a mess if nobody gets involved in matters beyond their own immediate business.

Mrs. Murphy took her hand off my shoulder, smiling rather awkwardly. "I'm afraid I'm getting too old to be in charge of young children," she said. "I've given the Fosters my notice, as soon as they can find another housekeeper."

I didn't tell her I was glad, of course, but I was. I hoped the next housekeeper would be better for the kids. "I got to like them, quite a lot," I told her, and to my surprise, I meant it.

Mrs./Dr. Foster overheard that. Though her eyes were puffy from crying, she was smiling. "It sounds as if they've become rather fond of you, too. How'd you like a job for the rest of the summer, spending days with them when their father and I can't be at home? Just keeping them entertained?"

I drew in a deep breath. Such a short time ago I'd thought I'd be glad to be done with baby-sitting the Foster kids.

"They need someone they like," Mrs./Dr. Foster

said. "Someone who really cares about them. We'll give you a raise, of course. And a reward, for the way you took care of them during this kidnapping business."

I swallowed and stuck my neck out, the way Tim's always telling me not to do. "Sure. I guess I could do that. Only I have some sort of strong feelings about them—that they need more attention from their parents, as well as from a sitter."

My heart was beating hard, because it really wasn't any of my business, and maybe she'd take back the offer of a job.

Mrs./Dr. Foster didn't cut me down, though, the way I sort of expected her to do. Instead, she smiled.

"We'll have to discuss that, won't we? I had a lot of time to think, while the children were missing. And I realized that we weren't spending enough time with them, either one of us. You will come tomorrow, won't you, and we'll talk about it?"

"All right," I agreed.

And then Shana tugged at my fingers. "I hafta go potty," she said, as she'd said so many times before.

When Mrs./Dr. Foster laughed, there were tears in her eyes.

"I guess you're hired, then, Darcy," she told me. "I'll take you to the bathroom, Shana."

"Come on, let's go home," my dad said, wrapping an arm around my shoulders. "I called your mother and told her you were safe, but she probably won't believe it until she sees you."

So we went out and got in our car and went home.

"Somebody'll have to take care of the dogs, until Okie comes home from the hospital," I told my dad. "Maybe I ought to be the one to do it. They'll let me feed them now."

"Good," Dad said. "You can get Tim to run you out there every day. I'm surprised you were able to make friends with a pair of guard dogs."

"I think they were Okie's pets as much as guard dogs," I said. "They'd gotten used to his granddaughter; and the kidnappers didn't like them, so the dogs never got friendly with *them*."

I couldn't wait to tell Irene all about it. I'd finally had an experience that Irene hadn't had, and neither had anybody else we knew. Not that I'd ever want to go through anything like that again, but now that it was all over I was beginning to see what a good story it would make to tell my friends.

My mom cried when we walked in the door, the way I knew she would. She hugged me and asked if I was hungry; and I decided I was. I had a peanut butter sandwich and a glass of milk, and for once Mom broke her rule about no sweets between meals and let me have a piece of carrot cake, too.

While I ate, I called Irene, even though it was so late.

She'd heard the news on a TV bulletin, and she sounded awed. "What was it like, Darce? Did they hurt you?"

"No, we're all okay." I lowered my voice. "What's happened to Diana? Is she still in the tree house?"

"No. She came down after your mother found out she was there." Irene hesitated, then confessed, "I had to tell her. I mean, I asked Diana first, and she said I could. Your mom called somebody from the Child Protective Services, and they said there'll be a hearing Monday, to see if Diana has to go home or not.

They talked to her aunt in California, and it sounded as if maybe they'd send Diana there if there's evidence her father's been abusing her. Boy, after this, I guess that's all the evidence they need! Though he may not be around," she added. "So maybe she can just stay with her mother."

"Her dad's gone to the hospital to have his leg stitched up, and her brothers are both there, too, with about a million wasp stings," I told her. "I think Mr. Hazen heard her sister Ellen talking about the Fosters and their house after she baby-sat for them, and he thought it would be a good way to get some money without working for it."

"Yeah. Poor Diana."

I swallowed some milk and agreed. "It would be tough to know your father's a kidnapper. He won't be abusing her anymore, though. They'll put him in jail as soon as they fix up his leg. Clancy said it'll be for years, if Jeremy and I testify before the court the same way we told it all to him."

I guessed it would probably take all night to tell her everything about the kidnapping, and I had to report to work at the Fosters' in the morning.

Still, when would I ever have this kind of news to relay again? Never, I hoped, so I might as well make the most of it now.

It was way, way past my usual bedtime, and I thought my mom would say so; but she just squeezed my shoulder as she went past, smiling at me, with never a word about the time.

"Tell me every detail," Irene breathed.

"Just let me get another piece of cake first," I agreed, and made myself comfortable for a good long talk.